HARLEQUIN®
Presents

Enjoy eight new titles from Harlequin Presents in August!

Lucy Monroe brings you her next story in the fabulous ROYAL BRIDES series, and look out for Carole Mortimer's second seductive Sicilian in her trilogy THE SICILIANS. Don't miss Miranda Lee's ruthless millionaire, Sarah Morgan's gorgeous Greek tycoon, Trish Morey's Italian boss and Jennie Lucas's forced bride! Plus, be sure to read Kate Hardy's story of passion leading to pregnancy in *One Night, One Baby*, and the fantastic *Taken by the Maverick Millionaire* by Anna Cleary!

We'd love to hear what you think about Presents. E-mail us at Presents@hmb.co.uk or join in the discussions at www.iheartpresents.com and www.sensationalromance.blogspot.com, where you'll also find more information about books and authors!

D0680940

RUTHLESS

Men who can't be tamed...or so they think!

If you love strong, commanding men,
you'll love this miniseries.

Meet the guy who breaks the rules to get
exactly what he wants, because he is...

HARD-EDGED & HANDSOME
He's the man who's impossible to resist....

RICH & RAKISH
He's got everything, and needs nobody...
until he meets one woman....

He's RUTHLESS!
in his pursuit of passion; in his world
the winner takes all!

Brought to you by your favorite
Harlequin Presents® authors!

Miranda Lee

THE MILLIONAIRE'S INEXPERIENCED LOVE-SLAVE

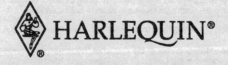

TORONTO • NEW YORK • LONDON
AMSTERDAM • PARIS • SYDNEY • HAMBURG
STOCKHOLM • ATHENS • TOKYO • MILAN • MADRID
PRAGUE • WARSAW • BUDAPEST • AUCKLAND

ISBN-13: 978-0-373-12748-1
ISBN-10: 0-373-12748-0

THE MILLIONAIRE'S INEXPERIENCED LOVE-SLAVE

First North American Publication 2008.

www.eHarlequin.com

Printed in U.S.A.

All about the author...
Miranda Lee

MIRANDA LEE was born in Port Macquarie, a popular seaside town on the mid-north coast of New South Wales, Australia. Her father was a country schoolteacher and brilliant sportsman. Her mother was a talented dressmaker.

After leaving her convent school, Miranda briefly studied the cello before moving to Sydney, where she embraced the emerging world of computers. Her career as a programmer ended after she married, had three daughters and bought a small acreage in a semirural community.

Miranda attempted greyhound training, as well as horse and goat breeding, but was left dissatisfied. She yearned to find a creative career that allowed her to earn money. When her sister suggested writing romances, it seemed like a good idea. She could do it at home, and it might even be fun!

It took a decade of trial and error before her first romance, *After the Affair,* was accepted and published. At that time, Miranda, her husband and her three daughters had moved back to the central coast, where they could enjoy the sun and the surf lifestyle once again.

Numerous successful stories followed, each embodying Miranda's trademark style: fast-paced sexy rhythms; passionate, real-life characters; and enduring, memorable story lines. She has one credo when writing romances: Don't bore the reader! Millions of fans worldwide agree she never does.

CHAPTER ONE

SHARNI was about to have lunch in a very trendy Sydney café when her dead husband walked in!

Her hands shook as they gripped the menu, her heart racing as she stared at Ray with shocked eyes.

Common sense finally kicked in, steadying her thudding heartbeat and whirling head.

Of course it wasn't Ray. Just some man who looked like him.

No, that was an understatement. A huge one. This man didn't just *look* like Ray, he was the spitting image of him. If she hadn't personally identified her husband's lifeless body five years ago, Sharni might have imagined he'd somehow not been on that horrible train that fateful day.

My God, he even walked like Ray!

Sharni's stunned gaze slavishly followed the man as he was shown to a table by the window, not all that far from her own. She kept trying to find something different, something out of sync with her mental memory of the husband she'd loved, and lost.

There was nothing.

Maybe this man was a little taller. And dressed a little better. That rusty brown suede jacket he was wearing looked very expensive. So did his cream silk shirt and smart fawn trousers.

Other than that, everything was the same. The same body shape. The same face. The same hair, both in colour and style.

Ray had had the loveliest hair: thick and wavy, a rich brown with a hint of red. He'd worn it longish, well down onto his shirt collar. She'd loved running her hands through his hair. He'd loved it, too.

Ray's double had exactly the same hair.

Sharni's mouth dried as she waited for him to sit down, waited to see if he would scoop his hair back from his forehead the way Ray had done every time he sat down.

When he did, Sharni only just stopped herself from crying out.

What cruel trick of fate was this?

She'd been doing so well lately, finally feeling capable of moving on with her life. She was working again. Okay, only part-time, but it was better than sitting at home all day.

This trip to Sydney had been another huge step for her. When her sister had given her a weekend package holiday in Sydney for her thirtieth birthday a couple of months ago, Sharni had initially shrunk from the idea.

'I can't leave Mozart for a whole weekend, Janice,' she'd said straight away, even though she knew this was just an excuse.

Admittedly, Mozart was not the easiest of dogs to mind. He still pined for Ray and could become snappy with other people. John, however—a local vet and Sharni's employer—had a way with the sad little terrier, and would happily mind him for Sharni.

Janice had seen through her excuse and worked on her quite relentlessly. So had Sharni's psychologist, a very kind lady who'd been treating her since she was diagnosed with post-traumatic stress a year ago.

Finally, Sharni agreed to go.

Getting on that damned train yesterday had been difficult, but she'd managed, though she'd grabbed for her mobile the moment the train had moved away from the station, fearing a panic attack coming on. Janice had calmed her down with some sympathetic but sensible talking, and by the time the train had arrived in Sydney Sharni had felt a little like her old confident self. Confident enough, anyway, to have her hair done first thing this morning in the hotel beauty salon before hitting the shops to buy some new clothes. Just casual ones, but more expensive than what she usually bought.

Money wasn't a problem, Sharni hardly having touched the three-million-dollar compensation payment she'd received eighteen months ago.

When she'd walked into this café shortly after one, dressed in one of her new outfits, her spirit had been much more optimistic, and her stomach free from anxiety.

Now, suddenly, her whole world had tipped out of kilter again.

She couldn't stop staring at the handsome stranger with his heartbreakingly familiar features.

Sharni had read somewhere that everyone had a double in this world, but this was way beyond being a double. If she hadn't known better, she would have said this man was Ray's twin brother.

Her mouth fell open at this last thought. Maybe he *was!* Ray, after all, had been adopted, and had never found out the circumstances behind his birth, saying he didn't want to know.

It wasn't unheard of for twins to be separated at birth and adopted out to different families. Could that be the solution to the startling evidence before her eyes?

She had to find out.

Had to.

CHAPTER TWO

ADRIAN had spotted the attractive brunette through the glass front of the café before coming inside. Despite his having a penchant for attractive brunettes, her presence had nothing to do with his entering. Since moving into his luxury apartment in Bortelli Tower a month ago, Adrian had become a regular at the ground-floor café, partly because of its convenience but mostly because the food was great.

The brunette had looked up when he'd walked in. Looked up and looked right at him. Hard.

At another time, Adrian might have encouraged her by returning solid eye contact, instead of averting his own gaze and pretending he hadn't noticed her interest.

Today, however, he was not in the mood for female company. He was still smarting over what Felicity had said to him last night.

'You should never have a real girlfriend,' she'd thrown at him after he'd been appallingly late for a dinner date. 'What you need is a mistress! Someone on tap who's just there for the sex. Someone you don't have to seriously care about, or consider. What *I* need is a man to love me with his whole heart and soul. The only thing you love, Adrian Palmer, is yourself, and your bloody buildings. I'm sick to death of waiting for you to ring me, or to show up. A good friend warned me about your reputation as a womanising workaholic, but I stupidly thought I could change you. I see now that I can't. So I'm out of here. Maybe one day you'll meet some girl who'll break *your* heart. I sure hope so.'

Being told he had a reputation as a womanising workaholic had shocked Adrian. So had the realisation that he'd hurt Felicity, whom he'd always thought was as career-orientated as he was. Obviously, she'd been more emotionally involved with him than he'd ever been with her.

He should have noticed, he supposed. But he hadn't.

He'd spent a sobering few hours last night, vowing to change his self-centred ways. Which was why he continued to ignore the brunette, despite his male ego being seriously stroked by the way her eyes followed him all the way across the room.

But when he sat down and scooped his hair back out of his own eyes, he caught a glimpse of her reflection in the window.

Wow, she wasn't just attractive. She was *very* attractive, with long glossy black hair framing a pretty face and big brown eyes, which remained flatteringly glued to him.

When he picked up the menu, Adrian couldn't help

slanting a quick glance her way. Her eyes immediately dropped away, but not before he saw embarrassment in them.

Thank goodness she wasn't the bold type, he thought, otherwise he might be tempted to go over to her table and ask her to join him for lunch. Which didn't say much for his resolve to mend his womanising ways.

The brunette's action of getting up from her table and approaching his totally surprised Adrian.

'Um…excuse me,' she said, rather hesitantly.

He glanced up from where he'd been pretending to read the menu.

She was even prettier up close, with a heart-shaped face, clear skin, a sweet little turned-up nose and a very kissable mouth. Her figure wasn't half bad, either, shown to advantage in superbly tailored black trousers and a fitted pink jumper, which emphasised her full breasts and tiny waist.

'I'm sorry,' she went on, 'but I have a question which I simply must ask you. You'll probably think it very rude of me, but I…I need to know.'

'Know what?'

'Are you adopted, by any chance?'

Adrian blinked up at her. As a pick-up line, this was a highly original one and very effective. Far better than the old 'Have we met somewhere before?'

Maybe he'd misread her earlier. Maybe she *was* bold. But with enough womanly wiles to be subtle in pursuit of what she wanted.

That was one of the reasons he was drawn to brunettes. He'd always found them interesting. And more of a challenge.

Adrian was a man who liked a challenge.

'No, I'm definitely not,' he replied, and wondered what she'd do now.

She frowned, her expression bewildered.

'Are you absolutely sure? I mean…I don't want to cause trouble, but some parents don't tell their children they're adopted. Is there any chance at all that you could be?'

Adrian finally appreciated that she wasn't trying to pick him up. Her question was genuine, evidenced by the distress in her quite lovely brown eyes.

'I assure you that I am my parents' biological child, and I have photos to prove it. Besides,' he added, 'my father would never have kept something as important as that from me. He was a real stickler for honesty.'

'That's incredible, then,' she said. 'Truly incredible.'

'What is?' he asked, curious now.

She shook her head. 'No matter,' she muttered rather dispiritedly. 'I'm sorry for bothering you.'

'No, don't go,' he said when she began to turn away. There was a mystery here to solve.

Adrian loved mysteries almost as much as challenges.

'You can't leave me up in the air like this. I need to know why you thought I was adopted. Sit down and tell me.'

She glanced worriedly back at her table where she'd left her handbag, along with several shopping bags.

'Why don't you get your things and join me for lunch?' he suggested.

She stared back at him for a long moment. 'I'm sorry. I…I don't think I can do that.'

'Why not?'

Her eyes grew agitated, as did her hands, their wringing action bringing his attention to her wedding and engagement rings.

The realisation that she was married disappointed Adrian more than anything had in a long time.

'Because your husband wouldn't like it?' he said, nodding towards her left hand.

Mentioning her husband seemed to agitate her more.

'I…I don't have a husband any more,' she blurted out. 'I'm a widow.'

Adrian found it hard to hide his satisfaction at this news.

'I'm sorry,' he said, and tried to sound sincere.

'He was killed in an accident. I…I identified his body. I…Oh, God, I…I have to sit down.'

She slumped into the chair opposite him, her pale skin having gone a pasty grey colour.

Adrian hastened to pour her a glass of chilled water from the carafe on the table. She gulped it down, after which she shook her head again.

'You must think me mad. It's just that you…you look so much like him.'

'Like who?' he said just before the penny dropped.

'Ray.'

'Your dead husband.'

'Yes. The resemblance is uncanny. You…you could be twins.'

'I see,' Adrian said. 'So that's why you wanted to know if I was adopted.'

'It…it seemed the only solution.'

'They say everyone has a double, you know.'

'Yes, yes, so I've heard. That must be the case here. But it was still a shock.'

'I can imagine.'

'Actually, now that I see you up close, your features are not exactly the same as Ray's. Some things are a bit different. I'm just not sure what…' Her head tipped to one side as she studied his face.

'How long ago was your husband killed?' he asked, thinking it had to be recent.

'Five years.'

Adrian frowned. Five years! And she was grieving still. She must have loved him a lot. Still, it was high time she moved on. She was still young, and very lovely. Very, very lovely, he thought with a familiar prickling in his loins.

'Ray was killed in a train derailment in the Blue Mountains,' she explained sadly. 'Several people died that day.'

'I remember that. It was very tragic. And preventable, if I recall rightly.'

'Yes. The train was going too fast for the conditions of the track.'

'I'm very sorry for your loss. Did you and your husband have any children?' She looked old enough to have had children. In her late twenties, or maybe thirty.

'What? No,' she said a bit brusquely. 'No, we didn't. Look, I…I think I'd better get back to my own table. I'm sorry to have bothered you. Thank you for the water.'

Adrian extended his right hand over the table towards her before she could escape.

'My name is Adrian Palmer,' he introduced himself. 'I'm an only child, son of Dr Arthur Palmer, general practitioner, now deceased, and Mrs May Palmer, one-time nurse, long retired. I'm thirty-six years old, unmarried and a successful architect. I designed this building.'

She stared at his outstretched hand, then up at his face. 'Why are you telling me all this?'

'So that I won't be a stranger. That is why you refused to have lunch with me, isn't it?'

CHAPTER THREE

SHARNI didn't know what to say. Because her refusal to have lunch with Adrian had nothing to do with his being a stranger.

'Oh, I see,' he said knowingly, his hand dropping back to the table. 'It's because I remind you too much of your husband.'

'Yes,' she choked out. And it wasn't just his looks. She still could not forget the way he'd swept his hair back from his forehead. Not to mention the way he walked, with long, loose-limbed strides.

Just like Ray.

'Is that such a bad thing?' he asked gently.

'Well, no, I guess not…'

'Now that you're over the shock of our physical similarities, I'm sure you can see lots of differences.'

His voice was certainly different. Ray had had a rather strong Australian accent. This man—this Adrian Palmer—spoke with a voice that betrayed a private-school education. Not plumy, but cultured and refined.

He also had a confident air about him that Ray had never possessed. Her husband had been a quiet, shy man whose emotional neediness had appealed to Sharni's nurturing nature.

It was ironic, however, that his double was an architect, the profession Ray had always aspired to but which he'd never felt he had the ability to enter. Instead, he'd become a draughtsman.

'Please don't say no,' his double said, and smiled a smile that was totally unlike Ray. It was a seductive smile, showing dazzlingly white teeth and an almost irresistible charm.

Sharni was surprised to find herself wavering. Maybe because, suddenly, he didn't remind her of Ray at all.

'It's only lunch,' he added, blue eyes twinkling up at her.

Ray's eyes had rarely twinkled, she recalled. They'd been quiet pools whilst this man's resembled a sparkling sea.

'All right,' she agreed before she could think better of it.

He was up out of his chair in a flash, getting her things before she could hardly draw breath.

'Been clothes shopping, have we?' he said breezily as he placed her carrier bags on the spare chair next to her.

'What? Oh, yes. I...I still have some more to do this afternoon.'

'Right.'

When he sat back down, he swept his hair back with his hand again, leaving Sharni speechless once more.

He smiled at her across the table. 'You'd better introduce yourself.'

'What?' she said blankly.

'Your name. Or do you want to remain a mystery woman?'

Sharni gave herself a mental shake. 'There's not much mystery about me,' she said with a small laugh. 'It's Sharni. Sharni Johnson.'

'Sharni,' he repeated. 'That's a most unusual name. But it suits you. Ah, here's the waiter for our order. Do you know what you want, Sharni, or would you like to take a risk and let me order for you? It's not too much of a risk, as I've eaten here several times before, haven't I, Roland?'

'Indeed, you have, Mr Palmer,' Roland answered.

'Very well,' she said, thinking to herself that Adrian Palmer's confidence bordered on arrogance.

'You like seafood?' he asked as he studied the menu.

'Yes.'

'What about wine? Do you like white wine?'

'Yes.'

'In that case, Roland, we'll have the steamed bream fillets with side salad, followed by the almond and plum tart. With cream. But first, bring us a bottle of that white I had the other day. You know the one. It's a Sauvignon Blanc from Margaret River.'

'Right away, Mr Palmer.'

Sharni had to admire his *savoir-faire*. It had been a long time since a man had ordered a meal for her with such panache. Ray had been a bit of a waffler when it came to deciding what to order in a restaurant. Making decisions had not been her husband's forte. That had been her domain.

Or it had once. Sharni's decision-making capabilities had disintegrated shortly after she'd won the compensation case. It was as though she'd stayed strong whilst she'd sought justice. But the moment the verdict had come down in her favour, she'd gone to mush.

Winning three million dollars compensation had proved to be a hollow victory, because all the money in the world would never make up for the loss of her husband and her beautiful little baby.

Still, life did go on, as Janice kept telling her.

Her sister would have been proud of her for not running away just now. Though she might be suspicious of Sharni's motives for agreeing to having lunch with Ray's double. Janice might think she was pretending Ray were still alive, and nothing had changed at all.

That was not the case. This man might look like Ray, but he was nothing like him in personality. The only time she could ever pretend he was Ray was if he didn't speak. Or if he was asleep.

'You really designed this building?' she asked once the waiter departed.

'I certainly did. Do you like it?'

'To be honest, I haven't had a proper look at it. I was walking past on this side of the street, smelt food, realised it was lunch-time and came in for something to eat.'

'After lunch, I'll give you the royal tour. I live on one of the upper floors.'

Lord, she thought. What a fast worker!

'I don't think so, Mr Palmer.'

'Adrian,' he corrected with another of those seductive smiles of his.

Sharni had to confess that she found his attention flattering. She also found him very attractive. Which was only logical. Ray's looks had been the first thing to attract her. Physically, he'd stood out in a crowd. It wasn't till she'd talked to him that she'd realised how shy he was.

That had appealed to her at the time. Nowadays, however, she would probably go for a more confident, outgoing kind of man, the kind who would look after her, not the other way around.

But she wasn't ready yet to leap back into the dating world, especially not with the dead spit of her dead husband. And *certainly* not with such an accomplished ladies' man.

Sharni knew a womaniser when she met one.

'I don't think so, Adrian,' she said quite coolly. 'Lunch is all I agreed to. Take it or leave it.'

He sighed. But it didn't sound like a defeated sigh. Sharni suspected he was already thinking of another tack to take.

The wine's arrival brought that confident smile back to his handsome face, reminding her not to drink too much. She'd gone through a stage a year or so back when she'd drunk far too much. Nowadays, she limited her alcoholic intake, having been advised that alcohol was not good for depression, which she fell into every time her thoughts dwelled on all that she had lost.

It had been too much to bear. First her husband, and then their baby. Oh, God...

'Penny for your thoughts.'

Sharni gritted her teeth as she glanced up, then reached for her glass of wine. To hell with being sensible, she thought, I need this drink today.

Adrian watched her sweep the glass up to her lips and take a deep swallow.

'They're worth a lot more than that,' she replied. Somewhat bitterly, he thought.

'I'm not sure what you mean there.'

She took another gulp of wine before answering. 'I was thinking about the compensation I received from the Rail Authority.'

'I hope they gave you a decent amount.'

Her laugh was very definitely bitter. 'They weren't going to. So I got myself a lawyer and sued them.'

'Good for you.'

'I was very lucky. My lawyer was brilliant. A woman. She was so incensed by my case that she gave me her services, *pro bono*.'

'That doesn't happen too often.'

'Jordan was wonderfully kind to me.'

Adrian's eyebrows arched in surprise. 'Jordan as in Jordan Gray of Stedley & Parkinsons?'

Sharni's wineglass stopped in mid-air. 'Why, yes. Do you know Jordan?'

'She's married to Gino Bortelli, the Italian business-man who commissioned me to design this building. It's called the Bortelli Tower.'

'Good heavens! When did all this happen? Jordan wasn't married when she represented me.'

'About a year or so back. It seems Jordan and Gino knew each other years before and ran into each other again by accident when Gino was up here on business. Just in time, since Jordan was about to become engaged to another man. Anyway, to cut a long story short, true love won out. They've not long returned from an extended honeymoon in Italy. But they don't live in Sydney. Their home is in Melbourne.'

'What a shame. I would have loved to catch up with Jordan.'

'I can give you their home phone number, if you like.'

'Oh, no. No, I wouldn't impose like that. I was just a client after all, not a close friend. But I'm glad to hear Jordan's happily married. I presume she is happy?'

'Very. She and Gino have a baby already. A boy. They called him Joe.'

'How lovely,' she said, her eyes going all misty for a moment. 'I'm so glad for her.'

'How much compensation did she get you?' Adrian asked. 'Or is that a rude question?'

'Three million.'

He whistled. 'That's a nice tidy sum. I hope you've invested it wisely.'

'It's safe.' Safe, sitting in a bank account that paid a reasonable rate of interest and had absolutely no risk at all.

'Do you still live in the Blue Mountains?' he asked her.

'Yes. On the outskirts of Katoomba.'

'So you're just down here in Sydney today to shop?'

'Not exactly. My sister thought I needed a little holiday. She gave me a weekend package at one of Sydney's boutique hotels as a birthday present.'

'You mean it's your birthday today?' What a perfect excuse to take her out this evening. If he could persuade her to go, of course!

'No. My birthday was quite a few weeks ago.'

'And you were?'

She slanted him a sharp glance. 'Now that *is* a rude question. You should never ask a woman her age.'

He smiled. 'I thought that only applied when they reached forty.'

'Not in my book.'

'Fair enough. So what do you do? Or don't you work any more?'

'I'm a veterinary assistant. But I'm only working part-time these days.'

Why was that? he wondered. Because she didn't need the money, or because she was still traumatised by the tragedy of her husband's death, or perhaps the subsequent trial?

There was something in her eyes when she mentioned the compensation that told him the trial had been just that. A trial. Adrian was well aware of how stressful it was to go to court over anything. He himself had had to sue a client once, and it hadn't been pleasant. How much worse when it involved the tragic death of a loved one.

Her air of sadness touched him. But so did her Madonna-like beauty. It was damned intriguing, the effect Sharni was having on him. He could not recall ever feeling quite like this. She brought out the gallant in him. More than anything he wanted to make her smile. Wanted to give her pleasure.

More like give yourself pleasure, a sarcastic inner voice piped up. You want to get her into bed. That's the bottom line. That's always the bottom line with you, Adrian.

Adrian frowned. Normally, he would agree. But not this time. This time, something was different. He didn't want to seduce Sharni so much as have the opportunity to spend more time with her. He wanted to get to know her. *Really* know her, not just in bed.

'I wanted to become a vet,' she went on, 'but my marks at school weren't good enough. I never was one to study. I'm a practical, hands-on kind of person.'

'I don't think it matters what you do in life, as long as you enjoy what you're doing.'

'You obviously enjoy being an architect,' she said, and he smiled.

'Does it show?'

'You seem a happy man.'

'I love my work,' he said. 'Too much, some people would say.'

Even his own mother thought he was way too obsessive.

But that was his nature. Adrian could never do things by half. When something interested him, he became consumed, body and soul.

This woman interested him, in ways no woman ever had before.

This in itself was intriguing. What was it about her that made her so interesting to him? Yes, she was very pretty, but he met lots of pretty girls. She wasn't super-clever, or super sophisticated, or super sexy, as Felicity had been.

Aside from being a brunette, Sharni was different from every woman he'd ever dated. They'd all been highly educated career girls whom he'd met through his work. Felicity had been a top interior designer. Before that, there'd been a female architect or two, a corporate lawyer, a computer expert and one super-smart marketing manager.

There'd not been one veterinary assistant who lived in the bush and blushed when caught in the act of looking at a man.

'You're staring at me,' she said in a low voice.

Adrian smiled. 'Well, that makes us even. You've stared at me a good deal today.'

His counter-attack clearly flustered her. 'Yes, but you know why.'

'Are you saying you only find me attractive because I remind you of your husband?'

She blinked her surprise at his directness. 'Who said I find you attractive?'

'Your eyes told me. The same way my eyes are telling you I find you attractive.'

Her cheeks went pink. 'Please don't flirt with me, Adrian.'

'Why not?'

'Because I...I can't handle it.'

'Are you saying I'm the first man to pay you this kind of attention since your husband died?'

'I haven't been with another man since Ray, if that's what you're asking. I don't go out. And I don't date.'

Her admission stunned Adrian. Five years of living by herself. Five years without male company, or sex of any kind. It wasn't natural. Or healthy.

'I find that terribly sad, Sharni.'

'Life is sad,' she said, and took another sip of wine.

'You are coming out with me tonight,' he stated firmly.

Her eyes widened before meeting his over the rim of her glass.

'Am I?'

There was enough wavering in those two words, and in her eyes, to satisfy Adrian.

'Absolutely,' he said, just as their meals arrived.

CHAPTER FOUR

'COFFEE or tea?' Adrian asked.

Sharni looked up from where she'd been devouring the last bite of the simply delicious almond and plum tart.

Roland was standing by their table, patiently waiting for her decision.

'Coffee, please,' she said after dabbing her mouth with the white linen serviette. 'Cappuccino.'

'I'll have a short black,' Adrian told the waiter who swiftly departed to do their bidding.

Sharni could see why Adrian came here often. Not only was the food great, but the service was very quick.

'So where would you like me to take you tonight?' he asked.

Sharni sighed. She should have known he'd come back to that sooner or later. He'd very cleverly lulled her into a false sense of security over their meal by stopping the flirtatious talk and steering any conversation onto more impersonal topics such as food, politics and the weather.

Now, his eyes were back on hers again, their focus disturbingly intense. But oh-so-flattering.

He was right. She did find him attractive. How could she not? But Adrian's charm for her was not just physical. It was the way he made her feel, as if he found her the most fascinating female in the world.

There was no use pretending she didn't want to go out with him tonight. But the prospect was accompanied by a measure of fear. What if he tried to seduce her? What if he succeeded?

For the last five years Sharni had lived a sexless existence, that part of her body having totally shut down. She hadn't had a period since she'd lost her baby, various doctors suggesting her lack of hormonal activity was caused by shock and grief. To be honest, she hadn't given sex a second thought in ages.

Now, suddenly, she was very definitely thinking about it.

Was the wine over lunch to blame, or this man's amazing resemblance to Ray?

She'd been sexually attracted to Ray from the moment. But they'd dated for several weeks before they'd slept together. Even then, it had been left up to her to make the first move, Ray having been chronically shy in the bedroom department.

Not so this man, she thought as she glanced across the table. He would know all the right moves.

If only he didn't look so much like Ray…

'We could have an early dinner then go to a show

afterwards,' he said, breaking into her ongoing silence. 'Or a show first and supper afterwards, if you'd prefer. Have you seen *The Phantom of the Opera*? The musical, not the movie. They say this latest revival is better than all previous productions.'

Sharni had always loved the story of the phantom. She thought it highly romantic. Andrew Lloyd Webber's music was marvellous too, echoing the uncontrollable passions that consumed the main character.

'No, I haven't,' she admitted. 'But—'

'No buts, Sharni,' he broke in. 'Your sister gave you this weekend in Sydney so that you could enjoy yourself. It's not much fun sitting in a hotel room by yourself, especially on a Saturday night. If you're still worried about my being a stranger, then I'll ring Jordan right now so that she can vouch for me.' To show he meant it, Adrian pulled a silver mobile phone from his jacket pocket and flipped it open.

'No, no, you don't have to do that,' she said hurriedly. 'I can see you're not some kind of creep.'

His handsome face showed shock. 'I should hope not.'

'I suppose it wouldn't be much fun sitting in the hotel room tonight all by myself.'

'So you'll come?'

'You've talked me into it.'

'Fantastic,' he said, smiling.

Her heart fluttered. So did her stomach. He really was utterly gorgeous when he smiled like that.

'What about *The Phantom*?' he asked. 'Is that a goer, or would you prefer a different show? A play, perhaps.'

'No, no, I love musicals.'

'Would you like me to book dinner before or supper afterwards?'

'I think supper afterwards.'

'That's great,' he said with a satisfied glint in his bright blue eyes. 'Now, after we finish our coffee, I'm going to take you across the street to a spot where you can have a proper look at my pride and joy. Then, after you've been suitably impressed with my brilliance at designing the outsides of the building, I'll give you a quick tour of the inside.'

'It'll have to be very quick,' she told him. 'I'll need some time before the shops close to buy a suitable outfit to wear tonight. I only bought casual clothes this morning.'

'I could come shopping with you, if you like?'

Sharni could see he was very much a takeover type of person. 'Don't you have something else you should be doing this afternoon?'

'Not really,' he said. 'I finished my latest plan to my satisfaction late yesterday. I always give myself a complete break between projects.'

'For how long?'

'At least a day,' he said, laughing. 'So what do you say? I have good taste in women's clothes.'

'I hate taking anyone clothes shopping with me,' she said quite truthfully. 'I prefer to trust my own taste.'

'And an excellent taste it is, too,' he complimented, his gaze admiring as he looked her up and down.

Sharni could not help smiling. 'I think you are an incorrigible charmer.'

'And I think you could do with a bit of charming. Ah, our coffee's coming.'

'Just as well. I need sobering up. I think I'm a little tipsy.' It wasn't like her to feel this light-hearted. Or this happy.

Once they'd finished their coffee, Adrian saw to the bill whilst Sharni picked up her shopping bags and stood up.

Oh, dear, she thought when her head whirled alarmingly. There was no doubt about it. She'd had *way* too much to drink!

CHAPTER FIVE

'OH, MY!' Sharni exclaimed. 'That is one magnificent building.'

They were standing together on the pavement across the street, Adrian holding her shopping bags whilst Sharni shielded her eyes from the sun's rays and gazed up at Bortelli Tower.

'I never imagined anything this big, or this beautiful!' she said with ego-stroking awe in her voice. 'I love the grey colour of the glass you've used.'

'The manufacturer calls it smokescreen. Naturally no UV rays can get through. Or heat, or cold.'

'It's gorgeous. And the hexagonal shape is just so unusual.'

'I like it.'

She smiled up at him. 'I dare say you do, since *you* designed it. How many floors are there?'

'Twenty-five. The first ten are devoted to office space. There's a health club and heated pool on the eleventh floor. After that, it's all privately owned apartments, with lots of balconies to take advantage of the views.'

'I bet they're very expensive.'

'They are. But Gino sold every one of them off the plan.'

'Wow! That's incredible. So what floor do you live on?'

'The twenty-fifth.'

'The twenty-fifth.' She frowned momentarily before gaping up at him. 'You live in the *penthouse*?'

Adrian loved her sweet surprise. 'It was part of the contract I made with Gino when he commissioned my services.'

'But a penthouse right in the middle of Sydney has to be worth millions! I didn't realise architects got paid that much.'

'Some of us do,' he replied, thinking of the seven-figure fee he usually commanded for this type of job. 'But Gino asked me to oversee the construction of the building as well, so the penthouse came as a bonus.'

'Do you do that kind of job often?'

'Sometimes. It's great watching my designs take shape. But projects of this scale take a special sort of commitment. That's why I was able to negotiate such a good deal with this one. Come on, let's go back over the road and I'll take you up onto the rooftop. The view from up there is incomparable on a clear winter's day.'

'Will that take long?' she asked. 'It's getting on for two-thirty.'

'I could have you up there in five minutes,' he said. 'And back down here shopping in fifteen, tops. All the lifts are the latest high-speed design.'

She still hesitated.

Adrian understood why. Sharni was a nice girl. And nice girls didn't swan up to a man's apartment within a couple of hours of meeting him. Not even if that apartment was a penthouse worth millions.

'I promise I won't make a pass, if that's what you're thinking,' he reassured her. 'I just want to show you the view.'

This was only partly true. What he actually wanted, more than anything, was the opportunity to spend a little more time with her. She delighted him as no woman had ever delighted him. It was a serious shame that she wouldn't let him go shopping with her. He would have loved helping her choose the right outfit for tonight. A sexy little black dress, perhaps. With long tight sleeves, a short, bottom-hugging skirt and a low-cut neckline. Very low. The kind of neckline that needed a decent bust to show it off. Like the one Sharni had.

Adrian gave himself a mental shake when his train of thought began transferring messages to his body. Highly arousing messages.

Thank goodness it was winter and he was wearing a jacket.

His sudden upsurge in testosterone, however, urged him to take more control of this situation.

'Come on,' he said firmly, cupping his free hand

around her elbow and steering her back towards the pedestrian crossing at the corner.

She didn't protest, he noted, going along with what he wanted. As a woman sometimes did when a man took the helm.

'This way,' he said once they reached the kerb, and led her along the street frontage towards the main entrance of the building. On the way, they had to pass two shops, one of which was a very exclusive ladies' fashion boutique.

As luck would have it, there, on a mannequin in the window, was an outfit that was absolutely perfect for going to the theatre. It wasn't totally black. Only the skirt, which fell in floaty folds to mid-calf length. The top was purple, and beaded, with three-quarter sleeves and a deep, crossover neckline, which was subtly sexy.

Not so subtle were the black five-inch heels that the window-dresser had put on the model's feet.

'Oh!' Sharni exclaimed, and ground to an admiring halt in front of the window.

'You'd look good in that,' Adrian said straight away.

More than good, but he didn't want to gush. Women didn't like men who gushed.

'You really think so?'

'I really think so,' he said coolly. 'Let's go inside and you can try it on.'

CHAPTER SIX

SHARNI looked at herself in the dressing-room mirror and thought, Wow, I really do look good, just like Adrian said I would.

Not just good, Sharni amended as she turned this way and that, setting the black chiffon skirt swinging around her legs. I look sexy.

And I *feel* sexy.

Was it the wine she'd drunk over lunch? Or because the salesgirl had suggested she take off her bra?

Sharni's curves rarely went without support, despite their not being saggy in any way. She'd never been inclined to show off her breasts in public, Ray having always liked her conservative way of dressing.

What would he think if he saw you in this top? Sharni wondered as she stared at her exposed cleavage.

He'd be shocked, she knew. Shocked and disapproving.

She felt shocked, too. Not by the way she looked, but by the way she felt.

Unbearably excited.

A tap on the dressing-cubicle door sent a nervous gasp punching from her lips. 'Yes?'

'Your husband wants you to come out and show him what you look like,' the salesgirl called through the door.

Sharni should have denied he was her husband. But she didn't.

Instead, she swallowed, then opened the door.

'Oh, no,' the salesgirl said, glancing down at her stockinged feet. 'You can't go out there like that. I'll get you some shoes. What size are you?'

'Seven.'

'In that case the ones on the model should fit you. Wait here. I'll go get them.'

The shoes were produced, with Sharni having to sit down to put them on. They were cripplingly high and sinfully sexy, each having a narrow strap across the front, with two more straps attached at the back which wound round her ankles and tied in a bow. She'd never in her life worn anything like them.

Sharni teetered at first when she stood up, having to keep her steps small as she made her way very slowly out to where Adrian was waiting, leaning against a counter in the middle of the boutique.

He straightened on seeing her, his blue eyes narrowing as they raked over her from top to toe.

Never had any man looked at her in quite that way before, not even Ray. The intensity of his gaze overwhelmed her, making her knees go to jelly.

'Walk up and down a few times,' Adrian commanded

in that masterful way that made Sharni's stomach flutter wildly.

Not a totally unknown state for her these days. But her nervous tummy was usually due to anxiety, not excitement.

Once she found her balance, her hips surprised her by developing a decidedly sexy sway. The effect on her psyche was amazing. Suddenly, she was a *femme fatale*; a temptress who commanded all male eyes be upon her.

But there was only one male Sharni wanted looking at her at that moment. And he very definitely was, with glittering blue eyes that evoked a heat in her that felt both shameful and shameless.

'I told you you'd look great in that,' he said, his voice low and sexy.

Sharni's heart quickened its beat.

'She'll take it,' he told the salesgirl before Sharni had a chance to come to a decision.

'The shoes as well?' the girl asked Adrian.

'Absolutely,' came his crisp reply.

'You…you do realise I'll probably never ever wear these shoes again,' she said, even as she admired them.

'Of course you will,' he countered. 'Every time you wear that fantastic outfit. Now go get changed, like a good girl, while I fix up the bill.'

Sharni flushed with the weirdest mixture of pleasure and embarrassment. 'I can't possibly let you pay for my clothes, Adrian,' she protested. 'It's not right.'

'What's not right about it? I can well afford a few hundred dollars.'

'That's not the point!'

He smiled, then reached out to stroke a tender fingertip down her nose. 'All right, sweet Sharni,' he said, his eyes soft on hers. 'You can pay for your own clothes. But this is the last time you get to pay for anything when you're with me. Off you go and change now. But don't be too long. Now that you have something suitable to wear tonight, you don't have to waste the afternoon shopping. We can spend it together, doing something more interesting.'

He was like a steamroller, Sharni thought as she changed back into her trousers and jumper.

But it was exciting, being swept along like this.

What did he have in mind for this afternoon? she wondered momentarily before deciding she wouldn't wonder. Or worry. About anything. Not even what it was about her that interested him.

After all, a man like Adrian would have no shortage of women—more beautiful than herself—throwing themselves at him.

This last thought did give Sharni something to worry about. Surely Adrian must have a girlfriend. Surely!

Should she ask him and risk bringing an abrupt ending to their time together today? Or avoid the question altogether?

Sharni was still dithering over this dilemma when she emerged from the dressing room.

* * *

Adrian's satisfaction at the way things were going was temporarily derailed when he saw the expression on Sharni's face.

He didn't like whatever was going on in her mind, but didn't say a word whilst she paid for her purchases. Experience had taught him never to tamper with a woman's mind. They were minefields that could blow up in your face when least expected.

'Let me take a couple of those,' she said when they left the shop with him carrying all her parcels.

'If you insist,' he returned, thinking he would need a hand free to extract his key-card for the lifts.

'I insist,' she said, and took the two bags from the boutique.

They walked in silence over to the main entrance to the tower.

'This way,' Adrian said, the automatic doors opening when he stepped forward onto the entry mat.

Their reflection in the glass, however, showed that Sharni had ground to a halt behind him, that worried look still on her face.

Gritting his teeth against a flash of irritation, he turned and rejoined her on the pavement. 'What is it?' he asked. 'What's wrong?'

'I...I have to ask you something.'

'What?'

'Is there anyone in your life who would be upset with you taking me out tonight?'

'A girlfriend, you mean.'

'Yes,' she said, her eyes fixed unswervingly on his.

Man, but she would be a difficult person to lie to. Not that he had to, thank God. Felicity was definitely no longer his girlfriend.

'Absolutely not.'

If anything, her frown increased with his answer. 'I...I do find that hard to believe.'

Adrian's frustration was tempered by the flattery within her statement. 'There was someone till recently,' he said, but refrained from saying how recently. 'Let me assure you that there's no one who could object to my taking you out tonight.'

Her sigh showed genuine relief. 'That's good, then.'

'And if I'd said there *was* someone?' he couldn't resist asking.

Adrian empathised with the flash of indecision that crossed her face, because it echoed his feelings for her. Never in his life had he felt this strongly about a woman within hours of meeting her. He'd been attracted at first sight in the past. But this was more than that.

If there'd been some new man in Sharni's life, he would still have pursued her.

'No need to answer that,' he went on before she could put her obviously muddled thoughts into words. 'It was a silly question. Come on. I want to get you upstairs while the sun's still shining.'

CHAPTER SEVEN

SHARNI TRIED to relax during the ride up to the twenty-fifth floor, but it was impossible. Something had taken possession of her when she'd paraded herself in front of Adrian in that sexy outfit, something that she'd pushed to one side when she'd changed back into her less sexy clothes, but which had emerged with a vengeance once she discovered Adrian didn't have a girlfriend.

That something was desire. The desire to be kissed, and touched, and made love to.

Not since Ray had she met a man who'd made her feel remotely like this. Of course, Adrian did look exactly like Ray, which could explain the heat washing through her. Her body could be reacting to old tapes.

But somehow, Sharni wasn't convinced. The sexual hunger consuming her body at this moment was much more intense than anything she'd felt with Ray. When Adrian asked her what she would have done if he'd said he did have a girlfriend, Sharni had been shocked by the realisation that she would still have come up here with him.

He'd promised not to make a pass. Yet she wanted him to. Quite desperately.

The lift whizzed to a halt on the twenty-fifth floor in no time at all, Sharni having no space to come to terms with the shockingly aroused state she was in.

When the lifts doors opened an extremely tense Sharni followed Adrian into an elegant, marble-floored foyer, which had a domed ceiling and a spectacularly modern chandelier hanging from it. Straight ahead were double French doors through which she could see a huge and equally elegant living area.

'Put your parcels down here,' Adrian suggested, placing the ones he was carrying beneath a glass-topped hall table on their right.

She did so, then immediately asked him where the bathroom was.

Suddenly, she needed to go. Quite badly.

'That's the guest powder room,' he said, indicating a door on her left. 'When you're finished go on through into the lounge room and make yourself comfortable. I'll join you shortly,' he said, turning away and leaving her through the French doors.

The powder room had everything a multi-million-dollar penthouse would have: marble floors and walls, stylish firings and gold taps.

After she'd washed her hands, Sharni spent a couple of extra minutes combing her hair and refreshing her pink lipstick, all the while struggling to find some composure.

'I *look* the same as the girl who left the beauty salon this morning,' she said agitatedly to the reflection in the mirror. 'But I don't *feel* the same.'

Meeting Adrian had changed her. In ways she had yet to appreciate, or understand.

All Sharni knew was that she wanted Adrian as she had never wanted Ray.

This admission brought a wave of guilt. Because she'd had a good sex life with her husband, who'd been a gentle and considerate lover. On top of that, she'd loved him very much.

She didn't love Adrian. She didn't even know him. Not really.

You didn't get to know anyone properly in a couple of hours.

No doubt he'd been presenting his best face to her so far today, impressing her with his decisiveness, his charm, and yes, the evidence of his material success. What girl wouldn't be bowled over by a millionaire's penthouse in the middle of Sydney?

But did all that explain the sexual cravings that were currently consuming her?

Sharni shivered as she stared into her too bright eyes and flushed cheeks.

'What's happening to you?' she whispered.

Adrian waited impatiently in the living room for the powder-room door to open. In the end, he took off his jacket—the apartment was centrally heated—and draped it over the back of a chair, after which he started pacing around the room.

She was certainly taking long enough, he thought, his gaze continually darting her way. Finally, the door did open, but she was slow to emerge, moving over to place her handbag on the hall table before turning and walking even more slowly through the open French doors.

When her eyes met his across the room, Adrian immediately regretted his earlier promise not to make a pass.

Damn it all. Why had he chosen today of all days to play the gentleman? He never had before, not when he saw that look in a woman's eyes.

Sharni was just as attracted to him as he was to her, he was sure of it. Given the situation, there was nothing to stop either of them acting upon the chemistry sizzling between them. They were both adults, after all. Both free to do what they liked, in bed and out.

Such thinking fuelled the passion that was already simmering just below the surface of Adrian's cool façade. If only he hadn't made that rash promise.

As she came towards him her hip-swinging walk stirred his hormones further. His belly contracted as he struggled to get a handle on his increasing desire, Adrian reminding himself that at least he hadn't made any promises about tonight. He only had to wait a few hours and he'd be able to pull her into his arms and kiss her senseless without feeling like a total heel.

'You have a very beautiful place,' she said, finally

dragging her eyes away from his to glance around. 'You must have had it professionally decorated.'

'A decorator came with the deal,' he said. By the name of Felicity—that was how they'd met.

Frankly, he wasn't that thrilled by what Felicity had done. Her colour palette had been on the bland side: mostly pale, neutral shades with only the occasional touches of green and yellow.

He'd given her a totally free hand, because he'd already been preoccupied with his next project at the time the penthouse was being decorated. Now, he had to live with the results.

'It's lovely,' Sharni said.

'It'll do,' came his indifferent reply. 'Come on. Come out onto the terrace.' *Before I forget all my noble intentions and pounce!*

Adrian slid back the nearest glass door, stepped slightly to one side and waved her through.

She glanced up at him from under long lashes as she hurried past, her expression a tantalising mixture of femininity and fear.

Adrian's flesh reacted excitedly to both. Which rather shocked him. Why should her fear arouse him? Unless, of course, it wasn't *him* she was afraid of. What if she was afraid of herself? What if she, too, was being besieged with almost uncontrollable desire?

He followed her out onto the terrace, his mind in turmoil as his frustrated body began to create havoc with his conscience.

'Oh my!' she said breathlessly as she gazed, first at the rooftop pool and spa, then out at the view.

Adrian already knew it was a magnificent view, the penthouse's enviable position providing a wide panorama of the city, with Sydney's famous icons clearly visible: the Harbour Bridge, the Opera house and the Botanical Gardens, all of them bathed at that moment in the soft afternoon sunshine.

But none of them drew his eyes. Only her.

It was no use. His desire was too strong to deny. To hell with his promise not to make a pass. To hell with everything!

When he moved up behind her and cupped his hands possessively over her shoulders, her head jerked around to stare up at him with widening eyes.

'I'm sorry,' he said thickly. 'But I have to do this.'

Sharni froze as he turned her into his arms.

The surety that he was going to kiss her brought panic. Because she knew, if he did, she would be lost.

Her eyes pleaded for mercy but he ignored them, his left hand lifting to slide around her neck under her hair, his right hand cupping her chin, holding her face solidly captive in readiness for his descending mouth.

Her lips parted in a belated effort to voice a protest. But all that accomplished was to leave her mouth more vulnerable to his advances.

His kiss was far from gentle, in no way resembling Ray's kisses. Adrian's lips ground against hers, his kiss a branding on her mouth and *inside* her mouth. The forays of his tongue were aggressive and deeply sensual. Soon her head was spinning, her heart thudding loudly behind her ribs.

One kiss dissolved into another, then another, his hands dropping from her face to wrap around her back, crushing her against him. Her own arms responded by looping around his neck, her fingers entwining together, then pressing down to stop his head from lifting.

She didn't want him to stop kissing her. Not ever!

He didn't stop. He somehow managed to keep kissing her, even after he scooped her up off the terrace and carried her inside. By the time he lowered her to her feet—in the master bedroom, she was to discover later—Sharni's desire had moved beyond the need for just kisses. By then her body was sending messages to her brain for more intimate contact than mouth to mouth. She needed him inside her. And she needed him *now*.

Her mouth wrenched away from his, her desire-glazed eyes dropping to the black leather belt around his waist. It didn't seem shameless to undo that belt, just necessary.

Her fingers were clumsy with their speed. His, too. Together they stripped each other from the waist down, their carnal urgency having no patience with undressing any further than necessary.

Neither of them stopped to think once enough clothes had been removed. They fell onto the middle of the bed; he was on top of her. Sharni cried out at his rough penetration, a cry that echoed her desperate need. She didn't care that he wasn't gentle or considerate; she wanted him to pound into her. Wanted him to fill her to the utmost, over and over.

Which he did. Madly. Mercilessly.

It was wild and totally without thought. A raw, primal mating. An expression, not of love, but of the most primitive lust.

They came together, an experience that Sharni had never had before.

For an amazing length of time, her body was buffeted by twin pleasures: that of her own flesh spasming in helpless ecstasy, and the feel of his explosive, almost violent release.

The sensations were stunningly satisfying. Mind-blowing, in fact. Sharni was in seventh heaven.

Till Adrian muttered a four letter crudity.

All of a sudden, reality returned with a soul-shattering thud. Because what he'd just said was exactly what they'd just done.

Her eyes flew open to look almost despairingly up at him.

'Sorry,' he grated out.

Shame made her grimace, her head turning away as a distressed sound punched from her lips.

'Don't do that,' he bit out. 'What we just did, Sharni. It wasn't wrong. Foolhardy perhaps, since I didn't use a condom. But not wrong.'

Shock sent her head whipping back to face him. His

not using a condom simply hadn't occurred to her. But now that it had…

'Oh, God,' she sobbed, and stuffed a white-knuckled fist against her mouth.

'I promise you,' he reassured her hurriedly, 'that I do usually practise safe sex. God knows what happened just now, because it's never happened before. Things got out of hand. But I don't regret it. And neither should you. You needed that, Sharni. It's not healthy, going without sex for five years. The only problem I can see is if there's a risk you might fall pregnant. Is there?'

She couldn't speak. Just shook her head from side to side in the negative.

'Are you sure about that?' he asked, a frown in his voice. 'You said you hadn't had sex in five years, so you wouldn't be on the pill. Unless you are for medical reasons. Are you?'

Again, she shook her head.

'How long since your last period, then?'

'F…five years,' she choked out.

His eyes flared wide. 'Five *years*?'

Sharni groaned. Now she would have to explain herself and she didn't want to do that. But she supposed she had to, under the circumstances.

But not whilst he was still inside her.

'I…I need to go to the bathroom,' she stammered, and wriggled her bottom in an attempt to eject him.

'Liar,' he said, the weight of his body keeping her solidly captive beneath him. 'You just went ten minutes ago. What you need is to stay exactly where you are till I'm ready to make love to you again. For longer then thirty seconds next time.'

Sharni blinked up at him. Next time? He actually thought there would be a *next* time?

'But first, I want to hear about your not having a period for five years,' he stated firmly. 'Given the time frame, I presume it's connected to your husband's tragic death. So what is it? A post-traumatic condition?'

Sharni was stunned by his intuitive conclusion, even though it was only half her story. Not having to go into a lengthy explanation of her barrenness was a huge relief.

'Something like that,' she agreed.

'What do the doctors say? Will you get better?'

'Hopefully. Eventually.'

He frowned. 'That's really sad, Sharni. Which is probably what your problem is. You've been sad for far too long. What you need is to inject some fun in your life. You've made a good start, resuming your sex life. But you need a whole lot more where that came from,' he added with a wicked twinkle in his eyes. 'Come on. Let's get naked.'

Sharni could not believe it when he lifted up her jumper and peeled it up over her head.

'Mmmm,' he said when his gaze dropped to her white bra, which was comfortable but not the sexiest of undergarments. 'This will definitely have to go. In future, please buy front-fastening bras,' he went on when he discovered hers didn't have one. 'Or better still, stop wearing one altogether. You undo it, will you?'

It was a defining moment, his asking her to undo her own bra.

If she complied, it would mean she accepted his view of this situation: that having sex with him wasn't wrong. Plus, it was something that could be good for her.

The decision was taken out of her hands when he made an impatient face, slid his hands under her back and unhooked the clasp.

Sharni sucked in sharply as he drew the bra away from her breasts. How swollen they felt, with nipples that, she knew without glancing down at them, were fiercely erect.

'Oh, yes,' he murmured, and tossed the bra aside. 'No bra for you in future, beautiful Sharni.'

His hot gaze on her bared breasts sent a wave of heat flooding through her. She wanted him to touch them with the same kind of desperation she'd wanted him to be inside her earlier.

Which he still was, she remembered with a startled gasp when he grabbed her hips, pulling her hard against him as he sat back on his haunches.

'Wrap your legs around my waist,' he ordered her.

Another defining moment.

Impossible to turn her back on the pleasure that she knew awaited her with this man.

Her heart quickened when she obeyed him, her head spinning at the thought of her naked body spread before him like a virgin sacrifice on an altar.

She was helpless, his sex anchored deep inside hers, his hands free to caress her at will.

Dear heaven, but she was shameless with him. Utterly, completely shameless.

She lay there, hopelessly excited, whilst he undid the buttons on his shirt, then stripped it back off his shoulders. He had the same mat of dark curls in the middle of his chest that Ray had had, she noted. But Adrian was slightly larger all over and much fitter-looking, with well-defined muscles in his stomach and arms.

He was a bit larger everywhere, it seemed.

She'd only had a quick glimpse of Adrian's erection when she'd undressed him, but there'd been enough time to see that he was circumcised, another physical difference.

She found his differences oddly comforting. Not so his being totally naked in front of her. Her eyes travelled excitedly down the length of his torso, fixing onto where their bodies blended into one. His own gaze was riveted to *her* body, his eyelids heavy with desire.

'I've so been wanting to do this,' he said throatily as he reached forward to stroke his hand back and forth across the tips of her breasts.

Sharni bit her bottom lip in an effort not to cry out. How could such a simple thing tie her up in so many knots? Her nipples immediately felt twice as long, and twice as hard.

'Come here, you sexy thing,' he growled and scooped her up off the bed, leaning her back over his arms whilst his head bent to her chest.

She did cry out when he started licking a nipple, a strangled sound that was half moan, half whimper.

Oh, Lord…

When he sucked her nipple into his mouth, the muscles inside her contracted fiercely.

His head jerked up, his eyes dark and smouldering.

'No more of that,' he ground out, and lowered her back to the bed before shooting her a thoughtful look. Then he started touching her down there.

Her mouth fell open as her nerve-endings became electrified by his knowing caresses. Soon all she could think about was the burning pleasure of his touch, and the build-up of delicious tension in her body.

His stopping brought an agonised groan to her lips, her dilated eyes flaring wide as they lifted to his in frustrated bewilderment.

'I've decided you should wait a while,' came his coolly delivered explanation. 'Why rush things? We have all afternoon. Come on,' he said, and scooped her up off the bed. 'Let's go have a lovely hot shower together.'

CHAPTER EIGHT

JANICE glanced at the clock on her kitchen wall.

Ten past six.

She glared at the phone, which had been ominously silent all day.

'I'm going to kill that sister of mine,' she grumbled out loud as she attacked the onions on the chopping board. 'Ungrateful wretch!'

'I hope you're not talking about me,' her husband said drily as he came through the back door.

'You'd think she'd at least call, wouldn't you?'

Pete sighed. 'I presume you're talking about Sharni.'

'Who else?'

'You worry about her too much.'

'I know. I can't help it.'

Pete came over and rubbed his wife's very tense shoulders. 'Have you tried her mobile?'

'Several times. It just goes straight to her message service.'

'What about the hotel?'

'They say she's out.'

'Then she must be enjoying herself.'

'That'll be the day.'

'You never know, love.'

Janice sighed. 'I hope you're right.'

The phone ringing made her heart jump.

'That's probably her now,' Pete said.

'I certainly hope so.' Janice dropped the knife and hurried over to the kitchen extension.

'Hello?' she said as she swept the receiver to her ear.

'Hi. It's me. Sharni.'

'Sharni!' she exclaimed, throwing a relieved glance at her husband who smiled and walked off into the living room.

'I was just saying dreadful things about you to Pete,' she went on, but laughingly. 'For not ringing me, that is.'

'Oh. I'm sorry. I…oh, Janice! You've got no idea what happened today.'

Janice couldn't quite make out the tone in her sister's voice. Was she excited, or shocked?

Maybe a bit of both.

'Obviously not,' she said. 'Why don't you tell me?'

'I…I've just spent all afternoon in bed with a man,' Sharni blurted out.

The deafening silence that greeted Sharni echoed her own bewilderment at her highly uncharacteristic behaviour.

Sharni had always confided in her big sister, so Janice

already knew that she was not a girl to jump into bed lightly. She'd only had one serious boyfriend before Ray and none since. It simply wasn't in Sharni's nature to sleep with a man unless she thought she was in love.

Or it hadn't been, up till now…

'Really?' Janice said at last, surprising Sharni by not sounding too shocked. 'Well, I did tell you to enjoy yourself in Sydney. Still, I have to admit I wasn't expecting that. So who is this Casanova? And how did you meet him?'

Sharni sighed with relief that her sister was taking her news so well. 'His name is Adrian Palmer,' she said. 'He's an architect and a friend of Jordan. You remember Jordan, my lawyer?'

'Of course. So you'd met this Adrian before, had you?'

Sharni winced. If only she had…

'Well…no. No, I hadn't, actually. I…oh, golly, it's just so hard to explain.'

'Try.'

'I was in this restaurant, having lunch, when he walked in.'

'And?' Janice prompted when Sharni started waffling over whether she should tell Janice that Adrian was Ray's double. Or not.

'He…he asked me to join him for lunch.'

'He picked you up, you mean.'

Lord, but this was difficult. 'Well…sort of. But he did introduce himself properly first. And he did offer to ring Jordan and have her vouch for his character.'

'Mmm. Smart move. So how much wine did you drink over lunch?'

Sharni bit her bottom lip. 'About two thirds of a bottle.'

'That's quite a bit for a girl who's been on the wagon.'

'I don't think it was the wine, Janice. It was the man.'

'Wow! He must be really something to seduce *you* that quickly. So after lunch he took you where? Back to your hotel room?'

'No. We went to his place. But not straight away,' she hastened to add, hoping that made things sound a little less sluttish. 'We went shopping first. For a dress for me to wear out tonight. He…he's taking me to the theatre. To see *The Phantom of The Opera*.'

'Brother! He's a fast worker all right. And after the shopping?'

'We…um…we went up to the top of this building he designed. It's called the Bortelli Tower. Adrian lives in the penthouse.'

'The penthouse, no less! This is getting better and better.'

Sharni's eyebrows lifted. Janice didn't sound as if she was disgusted at all. In fact, she sounded almost…approving.

'I presume he's handsome as well as successful,' Janice rattled on in a bright and breezy voice.

'Well…yes. Very.'

'Then what on earth are you sounding so worried about?'

'There's something I haven't told you yet. Janice, he's the spitting image of Ray. I mean, the *spitting image*!'

Janice groaned a deeply disappointed groan. There she'd been, thinking Sharni had finally moved on with her life.

She should have known better.

'Please don't tell me you only went to bed with this man so you could pretend he was Ray.'

'No!' Sharni denied. 'No! It wasn't like that at all. Yes, he does look like Ray. Startlingly so. But in personality, he's as different as chalk is from cheese. What Adrian made me feel when he kissed me, Janice…it's nothing like what I felt when I was with Ray. To tell you the truth, I think I'm still in shock. The things I did with him, Janice. I'm blushing just thinking about them.'

Janice had to smile. The poor sweet love. Ray had been a nice man, but very shy and lacking in confidence.

Clearly, Ray's double had all the confidence in the world.

'So where are you now?' Janice asked her sister.

'I'm back at my hotel. I…I made the excuse that I needed at least two hours to get ready for our date tonight. But the real reason was I wanted time to think. And to ring you.'

'I'm glad you did.'

'You know, I thought you'd be disgusted with me.'

'Not at all. A little surprised, maybe.'

'Not as surprised as I was. I still don't know what

happened. I couldn't seem to control myself. I wanted him like crazy. I still do. What's happening to me, Janice?'

'Maybe you're falling in love again.'

'No, no, it's not love. It's wild and wicked. I'm not myself with Adrian. I'm someone else: a sex-mad stranger.'

'Not sex-mad, Sharni. A normal healthy young woman of thirty who's been alone too long.'

'That's what Adrian said.'

'Did you tell him about Ray?'

'Yes. Yes, I did. If you must know I was so shocked when I first saw Adrian walk into the restaurant that I went over to his table and asked him if he was adopted.'

'Adopted!'

'I had this crazy idea he had to be Ray's twin brother.'

'Oh, yes, that's right. Ray was adopted, wasn't he?'

'Yes.'

'I presume this Adrian wasn't.'

'No.'

'Still, he must look a hell of a lot like Ray to make you think that,' Janice said, even more convinced now that this was why Sharni had ended up in bed with him.

'There are some slight physical differences. And he's nothing like Ray in the way he acts. He's much more...um...'

'Confident?' Janice finished for her.

Sharni laughed. Not a sound Janice had heard often on her sister's lips during the past few years. 'I was thinking more of arrogant...and masterful.'

'Especially in bed.'

'Yes…'

'Sounds like exactly what the doctor ordered.'

'That's what Adrian said, too.'

'Mmm. You've told him quite a bit about yourself, haven't you?'

'Not everything…'

Janice knew what her sister was referring to. The baby. Sharni could never bring herself to talk about the baby. Not without crying…

'No need to tell him about that,' she said quickly. 'Let's face it, Sharni, love, this is probably only going to be a weekend fling, so there's no need to spill your entire heart out to the man.'

'You're probably right.'

'You sound unsure. Do you think he's serious about you?'

'I can't see why he would be. A man like him. He could have anyone.'

'Don't you dare put yourself down like that. You are a very beautiful girl, with the kindest nature and a good brain. Any man would be lucky to have a girlfriend like you.'

'You're biased.'

'Too bloody right I am!'

When Sharni laughed again, tears pricked at Janice's eyes. There'd been a time when she'd thought she'd never hear that sound again.

'Look,' Janice said after swallowing the great big lump

in her throat. 'Why don't you stop worrying and just lie back and enjoy the experience? There's nothing wrong with having a wild and wicked weekend with a man, provided he's nice to you. He is nice to you, isn't he?'

'*Very* nice.'

'Then go out tonight, have fun and whatever comes, comes. Off you go now and keep me posted.'

Sharni suppressed a moan as she hung up the phone.

She knew what would come tonight.

Being with Adrian *had* turned her sex mad.

Sharni still could not believe she'd allowed him such liberties with her body. There wasn't an inch that he hadn't explored, either with his hands or his mouth.

Her mouth went dry as an image flashed into her mind. That of herself in the shower with Adrian, her hands braced against the tiled wall, him behind her.

Shameless, she'd been, utterly shameless.

Yet she'd enjoyed every moment, hadn't she? No use being a hypocrite and pretending that she hadn't.

Sharni took some comfort from her sister's reaction. Janice didn't seem to think what she was doing was wrong.

Janice also didn't expect the affair to last beyond this weekend.

Which was only logical, Sharni supposed, even if it was a depressing thought.

If she was brutally honest, she didn't want her affair with Adrian to end. Not tomorrow. Not ever!

Because whilst she was in his arms, there were no

painful memories. There was nothing but the heat of the moment and the most incredible pleasure.

Sharni shivered, then glanced at the bedside clock. Six twenty-seven. In just over an hour she would be with him again.

An hour to make herself as beautiful as she could possibly be.

An hour to think about what her lover might do to her later that night.

The longest hour of her life.

CHAPTER NINE

ADRIAN found himself whistling as he walked the two blocks to the boutique hotel Sharni was staying at, a four-star establishment down near the Rocks.

He could not recall when he'd felt this carefree. Or this light-hearted. Certainly not over the last few years.

He'd mistakenly thought he was happy with his life and his career. But it had become obvious to Adrian today that his rise to fame as one of Sydney's wealthiest, most sought-after architects had come at a price. He'd lurched from one project to the next, never going on a holiday, never committing himself to anything that would take too much of his precious time.

Which was why his relationships never lasted.

Felicity had been so right to call him a womanising workaholic, because that was exactly what he'd become, bedding one brunette after another during the miserably small blocks of time he'd allotted for dating.

But architecture had been the last thing on his mind since meeting Sharni. His focus had been all on her, especially once he got her into bed. He could not seem to stop making love to her, especially once he realised how inexperienced she was. He'd wanted to show her everything, wanted to *do* everything.

And she'd been with him all the way. Delightfully, deliciously.

Okay, so she'd been a bit shocked a couple of times, and slightly hesitant once or twice. But not for long.

He'd kept her in bed as long as he could, only letting her go because he'd temporarily run out of steam. He was a man, after all, not a machine.

But the moment she'd gone, he'd missed her. Missed her warm presence, her soft voice, her sweet smile.

He'd showered, shaved and dressed with considerable speed, and now he was heading for her hotel, due to arrive a good fifteen minutes before the time they'd agreed upon.

But what the heck? He just had to see her again, had to kiss her again.

Probably not a good idea to kiss her too much, though. Hell, even *thinking* about kissing her was not a good idea.

Suddenly, Adrian didn't feel so carefree any more. Hot blood charged through his veins. Within seconds, he was as hard as the Rock of Gibraltar.

The thought of sitting in the theatre all evening like this was almost unbearable.

Adrian's teeth clenched hard in his jaw. Think about something else, you dummy!

Ah, there was the hotel, a three-storey, cement-rendered

structure of no particular style, which would normally have offended his architectural eye. But not tonight. Tonight, architecture could go take a flying leap!

He took the front steps two at a time, telling the rather portly doorman that he would require a taxi shortly. No problem, he was told. They came by all the time on a Saturday night.

'Excuse me, sir,' the middle-aged dragon behind the reception desk called out sharply when Adrian strode swiftly through the foyer. 'Are you visiting a guest? If so, I need to know who, and if you're expected.'

'Sharni Johnson,' he replied without stopping. 'In room nineteen. And, yes, I'm expected.'

Sharni was in the bathroom, titivating, when she heard the knock on her hotel-room door, the sound sending a shot of adrenaline racing through her already aroused body.

He was early!

Heart racing and head whirling, she hurried to the door, all the while trying to find some much-needed composure.

Whatever she was planning to say died on her tongue when she opened the door, Adrian's stunning likeness to Ray striking her once more.

Not that Ray had ever owned a pale grey suit like the one Adrian was wearing. It shouted designer wear, as did his mauve silk shirt and vibrantly purple tie.

Not many men could carry off such colours without looking gay.

But Adrian could.

'I'm almost ready,' she said at last. 'You're early.'

He didn't say a word, just stared at her for a long moment, then pulled her into his arms and kissed her with a passion that made the earth move beneath her feet.

By the time his head lifted they were somehow inside the room with the door shut behind them.

'Sorry,' he ground out. 'Didn't mean to do that. It's all your fault, you know. You do dreadful things to me.'

'You do even more dreadful things to me,' she countered, the provocative words tumbling from her still-tingling lips.

'I'd certainly like to,' he growled. 'I have to have you, Sharni. Right now. We have several minutes before we have to go. Would you mind terribly?'

Mind? She would die if he didn't!

When she blushed furiously, he groaned.

'You must think me very crass. I haven't even said how beautiful you look. Which you do,' he added, taking her arms and holding them wide whilst his eyes travelled slowly over her.

But then he groaned again. 'Hell, Sharni, I don't have time for gallantry. I'm like a rock. Here, feel me,' he bit out and pressed her hand against his erection. 'I can't possibly wait till later tonight. I promise I won't mess up your hair or anything. We'll do it like we did in the shower. Remember?'

She nodded, her mouth drying at the memory.

'This will do,' he said, and pulled her over to the writing desk in the corner.

'Hold onto this,' he commanded, and curled her hands over the back of the upright chair. 'Lean forward slightly.'

Her pulse rate galloped as she obeyed, her heart lurching to a stop when he flipped up her skirt, then yanked her pantihose down just far enough to expose her bare bottom.

'So beautiful,' he muttered as he slid his hands over her tensely held buttocks.

Sharni's hands tightened on the chair.

Adrian had a penchant for talking during sex, mixing orders with compliments, both of which drove her crazy with desire.

'No, don't,' he bit out when she tried to move her legs apart. 'Leave them together.'

She moaned when he eased into her. She wanted to push back against him, forcing him in deeper. But he held her hips captive with an iron grip whilst he rocked back and forth just inside her.

Gradually, he moved in deeper, then deeper still.

'Not yet, sweet Sharni,' he whispered when her thighs started to tremble. 'Wait. Wait.'

She could not wait. Could not think. She was out of control again, a helpless victim to the heat of the moment. And to him. She came with a rush, and so did he, his hot seed flooding her womb for ages.

When their bodies finally calmed, he pulled her upright, groaning as he slipped his hands inside her top to cup her throbbing breasts.

'We don't have to go to the theatre,' he suggested in a raspy voice. 'We could stay here. Order room service.'

The temptation to agree was intense. But at a crucial moment, Sharni glimpsed their reflection in the glass of the window behind the desk.

'I…I think we should go to the theatre,' she said, shaken by the decadence of their image.

'If you insist,' he replied thickly, but he made no move to release her.

Sharni swallowed. 'I…I need to go to the bathroom, Adrian,' she pleaded. 'Please let me go.'

When he did as she asked without further argument, Sharni bolted for the bathroom.

Ten minutes later, she emerged with her clothes in place and new lipstick on. But she still felt like a woman who'd been ravished too much in one day.

'You're not angry with me, are you?' he asked as they made their way down the hotel stairs.

'Why should I be? I could have said no.'

But of course, that wasn't true. She couldn't seem to say no to him, not once he started making love to her.

Uncontrollable passion was not a situation Sharni had ever had to deal with before. Sex with Ray had never been all that urgent. To be spun out of her head all the time evoked total confusion.

'I know what's bothering you,' he said as they reached the bottom of the stairs.

'What makes you think something's bothering me?'

His laugh was dry. 'Come now, Sharni. Your face is

an open book. But trust me when I say I'm not just using you for the sex.'

Sharni ground to a halt and stared at him. That thought hadn't really occurred to her. She'd been too busy, worrying about her own rather shocking behaviour.

When he reached out to lightly caress her cheek, her heart flipped right over.

'From the moment we met, I knew you were going to be something special in my life.'

A wave of relief flooded Sharni. A wave of sweet pleasure, too. Janice had been wrong. He didn't want just a weekend romp with her. It sounded like he wanted a real relationship.

The prospect was as thrilling as it was unexpected.

'I could say more,' he said, planting a tender kiss on her cheek. 'But if we don't get going, we'll be late. Come on, my darling,' he said, and took her hand in his. 'The Phantom awaits.'

CHAPTER TEN

HE REALLY cares about me, Sharni kept thinking as the taxi wove its way through the city streets.

What had been a big problem in her head—the uncontrollable passion and raunchy sex—suddenly seemed all right. Adrian's hand in hers brought a warm fuzzy feeling to her stomach. His side pressed against hers felt protective, rather than provocative.

She didn't speak, just leant her head against his shoulder.

They arrived at the theatre just in time, the curtain going up within seconds of being seated, leaving Sharni no time to ask Adrian how he'd managed to secure a booking at the last minute. Then, once the show started, she was so captivated, so enthralled, that nothing existed for her but what was being played out on that stage.

It soon became obvious why *The Phantom* was such a popular musical all over the world. The combination of a bitter-sweet romance with magnificent melodies and sets of visual splendour were a sure fire recipe for success. The touches of humour were great, too. Sharni laughed several times.

The intermission annoyed her, however. She didn't want the story to stop. She wanted to see it through to the end in one sitting.

But she had no choice once the curtain dropped and the lights came on. Only then did she realise how great their seats were, right in the middle of the front row of the dress circle. Yet Adrian had only asked her to go at lunch-time.

'How on earth did you get such wonderful seats?' she asked. 'Were you just lucky?'

'Contacts, my darling,' he said, thrilling her again with this new term of endearment. 'I was the architect in charge of the refurbishment of this theatre. The owner was so delighted with the result that he granted me permanent access to his reserved seats whenever he didn't need them. He's overseas at the moment, so I suppose there was an element of luck in our being here. Though they say one's luck improves with hard work. It was a damned difficult job turning what was a dump of an old movie house into what you see tonight.'

'It's lovely,' she said, glancing around at the classy decor. 'Best of all are these seats. I love the black leather. Most theatres have simply dreadful seats.'

'Yes, I know,' Adrian said drily. 'I've suffered in them. I had a friend design these with comfort in mind and had them specially made. The leather is the softest available.'

'That must have cost a small fortune.'

'The owner will recoup the cost with people coming back time and time again. I also made sure there was a decent bar area where people can be served quickly during the intermission instead of having to line up ten deep, then spill everything as they try to weave a hazardous path through the crowd. Come on, I'll show you, and get us both some champagne at the same time.'

Adrian was right. The bar area was huge and extremely user-friendly, with plenty of staff serving the drinks. Eye-friendly too, with no glitzy mirrors or gaudy bits. The carpet underfoot was the same dark red that covered the theatre floor, the walls and ceiling painted black with recessed lights. Again, the same as inside. The effect was rich and relaxing.

'What did I tell you?' Adrian said as he handed over her glass of champagne. 'Quick as a flash. It's quality wine, too. Not cheap rubbish.'

Sharni smiled. 'I probably wouldn't know the difference.'

'You would, once you got a headache. Which is something we don't want you to get tonight.'

Their eyes met, with Sharni trying not to blush. But failing miserably.

He leant close and kissed her on her flushed cheek. 'I love it when you do that,' he whispered.

'Well, well, well!'

Adrian froze at the sarcastically delivered words.

Damn and blast. Felicity!

His stomach churned as he straightened, then slowly turned around. Because he already knew this wasn't going to be pleasant.

She stood there, her grey-blue eyes cold as ice as they flicked over Sharni.

'That's fast, even for you, lover,' she said in a droll tone. 'Or was she the reason you were so late for our date last night? I can see you're already shagging her, so don't deny it. He is shagging you, isn't he, sweetie?' she directed at a stunned-looking Sharni. 'Yes, of course he is. And doing it very well, by the look of things. Of course, Adrian does do sex well. When he has the time, that is.'

Adrian suppressed a groan. Of all the theatres in Sydney, she had to come to this one. Tonight. To a show that was booked out for months ahead.

This puzzling mystery seemed partially solved when a good-looking but middle-aged man approached Felicity with two drinks in his hands and a frown on his face.

'I think you're the one who had someone in the wings, sweetheart,' Adrian countered. 'And he's right behind you.'

Felicity didn't even blink. 'You don't honestly think I was staying home pining for you all the nights you stood me up, did you? Kevin's been in love with me for years. Something you know nothing about.'

'Felicity, darling,' Kevin said from a short distance behind her.

'Coming,' she tossed back before throwing a sneering look at Sharni. 'You should know before you get in too deep that Adrian has this thing for brunettes. So if you're thinking you're special, then think again. You'll go the way the rest of us have gone. Do yourself a favour, sweetie, and find yourself a man who loves you, not this self-obsessed bastard.'

It was a brilliant exit line, if this were a play and not real life, Adrian thought wretchedly as Felicity whirled and stalked off, taking the hapless Kevin with her. Adrian might have taken some comfort from discovering that Felicity was not exactly heartbroken over their failed relationship, if it hadn't been for the way Sharni was now looking at him. As if she'd been hit by a truck.

'Sharni,' he began earnestly. 'Darling…'

'Don't,' she said, her voice breaking. 'Don't call me that.'

'Let me explain.'

'There's nothing to explain. I'm not stupid, you know. I got the picture.'

'What you got is a twisted picture. Felicity's a bitch.'

'Is she? Okay, then answer these simple questions. Did you have a date with her last night?'

'Yes. But—'

'Yes will do,' Sharni interrupted sharply. 'She dumped you, didn't she? When you were late.'

Adrian sighed. 'Yes. But—'

'So when you told me there wasn't any woman who would get upset by your taking me out tonight, you lied.'

'I didn't think she'd be all that upset. It was over between us. Well and truly. During the last couple of months we'd only been out three, maybe four times. I hadn't been to bed with her for at least two weeks.'

'Oh my! Two whole weeks. An eternity. *Do* you have this thing for brunettes?' she snapped.

Adrian didn't like the feeling of being cornered. Why wouldn't she let him explain, instead of shooting off all these loaded questions, then never letting him elaborate properly on his answers?

'Look, we all have a physical type which attract us. You said yourself how much I look like your husband. It's the way things work with male-female chemistry. Just because you're brunette doesn't mean you're not special to me. Don't let Felicity's spite ruin things for us, Sharni.'

She began shaking her head at him, as though he didn't have a clue what he was talking about.

When the call came for them to return to the theatre, she handed him her glass. 'It was never going to work, anyway. I was a fool to think it could. Best we finish it right now.'

'No!' he exclaimed fiercely, bringing several startled glances from passers-by.

'Yes,' she said quite firmly. 'It's over, Adrian. Please don't make a scene.'

'Come back inside and watch the second half of the show,' he urged, desperate to persuade her to stay. All he needed was time and he'd make her see things differently.

'You really don't get it, do you?' she said. 'Your ex-girlfriend was right. You are a self-obsessed bastard,

Adrian Palmer. Now get out of my way. I'm going back to the hotel. By myself. Don't try to follow me. Don't try to contact me. I'm sure you've had several brunettes say this to you over the years. But I'm adding my bit for good measure. I don't want to see you ever, ever, *ever* again!'

CHAPTER ELEVEN

'CALM down, Sharni.'

'I can't calm down,' she sobbed into the phone. 'I'd like to kill him.'

'What you'd like,' her sister said, 'is to *not* have run into his ex-girlfriend tonight. Then you'd still be at the theatre, having a lovely time. Ignorance is bliss, especially with men like your Adrian.'

'You knew he was a womaniser, didn't you?'

'I knew he was a fast worker. That usually goes hand in hand with womanisers.'

Sharni groaned. 'He said I was special.'

'You *are* special.'

'He called me darling,' she wailed.

'You *are* a darling.'

'I thought he really cared. Oh, Janice! I don't think I'm ever going to forget him.'

'He was that good, eh?'

'What?'

'In bed.'

In bed *and* out, she thought despairingly, her fingers tightening around the receiver when she glanced over at the chair at the writing desk.

Shame curled around her heart as she realised just how easy she'd been with him. He must have thought all his Christmases had come at once. No wonder he hadn't wanted to let her go tonight. He'd probably been looking forward to another night of shenanigans.

'It's not the end of the world, love,' her sister said gently. 'Once you get over your indignation, you'll see that he was actually good for you.'

'Good for me! How can you say that?'

'Easy. Not only did he give you some great sex, he made you laugh, which is something you haven't done in a long time.'

'He made me cry, too.'

'Tears of temper more than true hurt.'

'You really think so?'

'He made you feel a fool,' Janice said. 'No woman likes that.'

Yes, he had, Sharni admitted. But he'd also made her feel beautiful and sexy and special and loved.

That had been his worst betrayal of all. She could have coped with his having had a girlfriend the day before he'd met her, if he'd just kept their weekend together strictly sexual.

But, no, he'd had to feed her a line of bull, hadn't he? Had to make her believe they might have a future together. That had been cruel and unnecessary.

It finally sank home that she was terribly naïve when it came to men of the world. Naïve and stupid.

Her involvement with Adrian reminded her of another salutary lesson she'd learned during the last five years: you could not rely on people to be just, or decent, or honest. The world was unfair and life was unfair.

But it went on, regardless.

The sun would come up tomorrow and she would somehow have to find the courage to go on. And the courage to go home. Which she had to do, first thing in the morning.

Because she could not stay here, in Sydney. What if Adrian contacted her tomorrow? What if he showed up at this very door?

She wouldn't put it past him. He was not the kind of man to take rejection lightly. He'd followed her outside the theatre when she'd stormed off, watching her closely as she'd jumped into a taxi. When she'd glared at him through the back window, he'd glared right back, his expression more frustrated than defeated. He probably thought he could still talk her round, once she'd calmed down.

Sharni could not trust herself with him.

'Would you feel terribly offended if I cut my weekend short and went home tomorrow?' Sharni asked her sister.

Janice sighed. 'I suppose not. But I don't want you moping around all by yourself.'

'I promise I won't mope. The house needs a good clean. I'll do that.'

'Why don't you catch a train up here instead of going home? Stay a couple of days.'

'I can't. I'll pick up Mozart tomorrow. I know he'll be fretting already.'

'Poor little dog. You know, he might benefit from a change of scene. We could take him. The boys have always wanted a dog.'

'No, I couldn't do that, Janice. He's all I've got left of Ray.'

'Mmm. Do you have an appointment with Dr Flynn this week?'

'No. I'm down to once every three weeks now. Look, I'm not about to do anything stupid, if that's what you think. I've used up all my stupidity for this week.'

'Don't be like that.'

'Like what?'

'Defensive. Can't you see I'm worried about you?'

'No need. I'm fine.'

A weary sigh came down the line, making Sharni feel guilty. She had a habit of saying she was fine when she was anything but.

'I'll ring you tomorrow night,' she promised.

'You'd better.'

'Love you.'

'Love you, too.'

Sharni hung up, lay down on the bed and stared up at the ceiling.

Twenty-four hours ago she'd been dreading this getaway.

Now she dreaded going home, dreaded looking at the photographs of Ray dotted around the house, and thinking, not of him, but of his double.

Part of her felt guilty over what she'd done, as if she'd betrayed her husband's memory. But her overriding emotion was despair that she would never feel again what she'd felt when Adrian had been making love to her.

With a strangled sob, Sharni rolled over and started to weep.

CHAPTER TWELVE

THE train ride home the following morning did not produce an anxiety attack. Crying for most of the night had left Sharni too tired for anything except just sitting there, staring blankly through the window.

She looked dreadful, she knew, with puffy lids and dark rings under her eyes. But who cared? There was no one she knew in the carriage, which was almost empty.

Rain started to fall halfway up the mountains, a bleak steady drizzle. Sharni grimaced as she realised the house was going to be freezing. Even if she lit the wood heaters as soon as she got there, it would be at least an hour before the air inside reached a comfortable temperature.

She really should sell and move. Regardless of how little she got for the place—small, weatherboard cottages on the outskirts of Katoomba were not in great demand—she had enough money to buy a house closer to her sister's home in Swansea.

Apart from the benefit of nearby family, the weather

was better on the coast. And there was the beach. She liked the beach, had grown up near one.

Janice had suggested this move to her several times over the past eighteen months, but she'd always rejected it, saying she couldn't bear to leave the home she and Ray had made together. Now Sharni saw that that had just been a pathetic excuse. The truth was she'd been too depressed to make *any* decisions, let alone a mammoth one such as selling and moving.

Suddenly, she couldn't wait.

She sat up straight in the seat, invigorated by the idea that cleaning the house today would have a purpose. *She* would have a purpose, a goal.

As though on cue, the train pulled into her station. Sharni grabbed her two bags and jumped off, eager to get home and get started.

Thankfully, her car hadn't been stolen from the station car park. Not an uncommon occurrence during the week, with people leaving cars there all day whilst they caught the train to work down in Sydney. It was a long commute—two hours—but more reliable than driving, especially in the winter. The roads were often slick with sleet, making driving hazardous and slow.

It took her five minutes to drive the two kilometres from the station to her home, which was situated at the end of a narrow, poorly tarred road.

Sharni frowned as she turned into the driveway.

Maybe it was just the rain, but the house looked terrible. As if no one had lived there for years.

'And no one has,' she muttered as she gazed with shocked eyes at all the evidence of her neglect.

There were weeds growing out of the gutters. The outside walls needed painting. The garden beds were overgrown and the browned-off, straggly lawn hadn't been mown in months.

It hadn't been like that when Ray had been alive. The place had been beautiful, like something out of a romantic movie, with a white picket fence and roses trailing over the iron archway that framed the front steps. Now the fence was a mouldy grey, with several loose palings. As for the climbing rose bushes...

They'd died, because she'd forgotten to water them.

Ray would have been devastated to see it like this, Sharni conceded sadly.

'Oh, Ray, I'm so sorry. About everything. I've let you down.'

But instead of succumbing to another bout of useless weeping, Sharni vowed to do something about it. She could paint, couldn't she? And mow lawns and pull out weeds. Maybe not today, since it was raining. But that didn't stop her from attacking the inside, which she suspected was almost as neglected as the outside.

If nothing else, all this activity would distract her from thinking about a certain person.

With house keys in hand, Sharni jumped out of the car and raced through the rain towards the front veranda.

* * *

'About bloody time,' Adrian muttered when he finally reached Katoomba shortly after three in the afternoon.

As drives went, that one was a doozy. The combination of continuous rain and curving roads meant his concentration couldn't flag for a moment, or his extremely expensive yellow Corvette would have gone over a cliff, or up the back of a truck.

It was a relief that Sharni had taken the train home, the only information he'd been able to get out of that dragon at the hotel.

'I'm sorry, sir,' she'd said with a sniff when he'd asked for Sharni's address or phone number. 'But the lady said I wasn't to give out her personal details to anyone.'

Adrian had been seriously frustrated, till he remembered that Sharni had been Jordan's client.

Jordan had finally supplied Sharni's address and home phone number, which thankfully had been still in her computerised files. But only after she'd quizzed him on why he wanted them.

He'd explained how he'd met Sharni, mentioning his likeness to her dead husband. He hadn't told Jordan about the sex, claiming instead that they'd exchanged life stories over a lovely lunch, but that Sharni had left afterwards to go shopping without giving him her phone number and address. He'd added—quite truthfully—that he simply hadn't been able to forget her and wanted to see her again.

When Jordan had warned him to go gently with Sharni, he'd promised that he would.

If Sharni let him, he thought as he drove slowly through Katoomba.

Adrian could not ignore the fact that Sharni wasn't going to be pleased to see him, especially since he hadn't rung to warn her that he was coming. He'd anticipated that she would have hung up without giving him a hearing. It wouldn't surprise him if she slammed the front door in his face as well. She'd been seriously angry with him last night. More angry, even, than Felicity.

When the taxi had sped off with her glowering at him through the back window, he'd been in two minds whether to go after her straight away, or not. In the end, he'd decided to let her calm down first.

He'd spent a wretched night, tossing and turning, upset that he'd hurt Sharni, when all he'd wanted to do was make her happy.

When he'd hurried to the hotel first thing this morning, Adrian had still been reasonably confident that he'd be able to talk Sharni round.

The news that she'd checked out had floored him. His inability to secure her phone number and address had infuriated him.

He'd brooded all the way home before a light had gone on in his head. She'd been *afraid* to stay, the same way she'd been afraid the day before.

He still wasn't sure if she was afraid of him, or herself. But either way, he wasn't going to let her get away. Because what he'd told Jordan was correct. He could not forget her. She'd got under his skin as no woman ever had before.

Adrian slowed the car even further once he left the centre of Katoomba, peering through the rain in search of the street on the left down which he had to turn to reach Sharni's house. He'd done a search of her address on the internet and printed off the relevant map, studying it before he left home. The trouble was distances looked different in reality than they did in maps.

The houses thinned. He crawled past a motel and a garage, wondering if he'd missed the sign.

No, there it was!

He swung the wheel left and drove slowly down the street, travelling a good way before turning into Gully Creek Road, which looked little more than a bush track. It had a narrow strip of tar down the middle and far too many potholes for Adrian's liking. Not too many houses, either.

The first one to have a readable number on the postbox was number eight.

Sharni's number was thirty-four.

He finally found it, right at the end of the road. There was a tidy white sedan parked in the driveway. But that was the only thing neat about the place.

Adrian's architectural eye found some pleasing aspects in the design of the house. He'd always liked colonial cottages with pitched iron roofs and verandas all around.

But they could look like dumps if they weren't well maintained.

Sharni's home looked like a dump. A deserted dump! He would not have thought anyone lived there if it hadn't been for the puffs of smoke coming out of the chimney.

As Adrian's shocked gaze took in the condition of the place and its surrounds he tried to work out why a woman who'd received three million dollars in compensation would live like this.

He found the answer with his own mother's behaviour when his father died a few years back. After the funeral, she'd gone into a serious decline, letting everything go. Her home, her garden, herself. Bills had not been paid and phone calls not answered. Friends had been turned away from the door. She'd spent most days in her dressing gown, sitting in an armchair and staring into space.

Her doctor had explained to her worried son that she was suffering from depression. He'd prescribed antidepressants and counselling but she'd refused both. This had gone on for over a year, at which point Adrian had stepped in and bought her a ticket on a world cruise. He'd virtually packed for her, put her on the boat and just left her there.

It had done the trick, her melancholy lifting after she met a charming gentleman on the ship who had shown her that there was still life to be lived, even at the age of sixty-eight. Their ship-board romance had not survived once the cruise was over. He lived in England and wasn't prepared to leave his roots. But Adrian's mother had come home a different woman, full of energy and ideas.

It occurred to Adrian that maybe that was why

Sharni's sister had given her a holiday in Sydney. To snap her out of her depression.

And it had been working, too. Till fate—and Felicity—had ruined everything.

The rain suddenly stopped, Adrian taking that as a good sign. He'd always been a positive thinker, having a cup-is-half-full rather than half-empty attitude.

He felt certain that Sharni had really liked him, the same way he'd really liked her. It was not just the sex, despite the chemistry between them being very powerful. If it were just the sex she would not have reacted to Felicity the way she had. That level of indignation and anger came from the beginnings of an emotional involvement. His own distress over Felicity's unfortunate appearance confirmed what he'd already suspected about himself: that he was on the verge of falling in love for the first time in his life!

Which was why he was here, determined not to return to Sydney till Sharni saw sense.

Climbing out of his Corvette, Adrian locked it, then strode through the open gate and up the weed-filled front path. He had to duck to pass under an archway that was covered in some kind of thorny bramble. Three stone steps brought him up onto the veranda. The front door had a tarnished brass knocker in its middle, which he lifted and banged against a brass plate.

The sound of someone knocking at Sharni's door brought a sigh of exasperation. Because at the time she was down on her hands and knees, scrubbing the kitchen floor. Also because she knew exactly who it would be.

Louise, from next door.

Louise was the only neighbour of Sharni's whom she would label a busybody. Most people who lived in the more remote areas of the Blue Mountains tended to keep to themselves, having chosen to live up here for the peace and quiet, the cooler air and the proximity to some of Australia's best bush walks.

When Ray had been alive, he'd given the woman short shrift. After his death, Sharni had welcomed Louise's seemingly kind visits for a while. But she'd soon come to realise that Louise's only interest in life was sticking her nose into other people's lives.

Unfortunately, by then, the infernal woman had been in the habit of dropping by at all hours of the day and night.

Fortunately, Mozart had upped and bitten her one day. Which had made her visits much less frequent thereafter. She also always came to the front door now, instead of just walking in the back door, unannounced.

Sharni suspected Louise had binoculars trained on her house most of the time. Because she always seemed to show up after Sharni had done something out of her usual routine. She would have noticed that Sharni had been away over the weekend. Also that Mozart wasn't at home. And she'd have spotted the smoke from the chimney, signalling her return.

The only surprise, Sharni thought as she rose to her

feet and threw the scrubbing brush in the sink, was that Louise hadn't come over earlier.

Sharni sighed as she made her way along the central hallway to the front door, not bothering to remove the scarf that she'd tied around her hair. Louise wouldn't care what she looked like. All Louise wanted was to satisfy her curiosity over where Sharni had gone and what she'd been doing.

As she reached for the door knob a small smile crossed Sharni's face. The old duck would die of shock if she told her what she'd been up to down in Sydney.

'Hi, Lou…'

The greeting died in Sharni's throat when she saw who was standing on her front doorstep. Adrian, looking dead sexy in blue jeans and a black leather jacket with a white polo-necked jumper under it.

For a split second, a wild thrill shot through her.

But it wasn't long before her overriding emotion was anger. Or was it embarrassment that he'd caught her looking such a fright?

'How did you find out where I lived?' she threw at him whilst she yanked the scarf from her hair. 'I told the hotel not to give out my address to anyone. Especially you.'

'Jordan told me.'

Sharni groaned. She'd forgotten they had a mutual acquaintance.

Still, never in her wildest dream had she expected Adrian to follow her up here. It was easy to walk over to a hotel a couple of blocks away from where you live, quite another to drive all this way on a cold, rainy Sunday.

She glanced over his shoulder to see a bright yellow sports car parked outside her house, sparkling with raindrops.

It annoyed her, for some reason, perhaps because it looked so incongruous, parked next to her tumble-down house.

More angry red spots heated her cheeks.

'What is it that you want, Adrian?' she asked, arms folding in front of her. 'If you've come for more sex, then you've come to the wrong house.'

Pity, he thought. Because he'd never wanted her more.

Her feistiness turned him on no end.

'I've come to apologise,' he said.

'For what? Lying to me, then shagging me senseless?'

Wow. This was a Sharni he hadn't met before. But he liked her even more than the sweet, vulnerable creature he'd met yesterday.

He should not have smiled. It was a tactical mistake.

'You listen to me, you egotistical bastard,' she said, unfolding her arms and jabbing the middle of his chest with a furious finger. 'If you think you can just show up here and I'll fall into your arms again, then you're very much mistaken. I admit you're good in bed. No doubt you've had a lot of practice. With any number of bru-nettes whose names you probably can't remember. But I don't aim to be your next playmate. Now get back in your fancy car and go back to your fancy penthouse, because you're not wanted here.'

'Really,' he said, all his good intentions flying out of the window in the face of her insults and that poking finger.

He grabbed her wrist and pulled her inside the hallway, swinging her round so that her back slammed flat against the wall. He ignored the alarm in her eyes, grabbing her other wrist and pinning her arms against the wall above her head.

'Let's see about that,' he growled just before his mouth crashed down on hers.

CHAPTER THIRTEEN

SHARNI'S lips betrayed her. They should have stayed firmly shut. Instead, they flowered open, welcoming the savage invasion of Adrian's tongue.

He pressed his body against her, squashing her breasts flat, his legs spread wide so that his hips were at the same height as hers. She felt his erection dig into the soft curves of her stomach, felt her outrage disintegrate as desire took over. She moaned softly into his mouth, the sound one of abject surrender.

His letting her go was as unexpected as it was by then unwanted.

Her arms dropped limply to her sides as she stared up at him.

'Don't you ever tell me again that you don't want me,' he ground out, his expression tight and angry. 'I could have you right here and now. The only reason I'm stopping is to show you that I'm not here just for the sex. I care about you, damn it. And I'm not leaving this house till you believe me,' he pronounced, stunning her further by moving over to fling the front door shut.

'I don't care how long it takes,' he added, turning to face her once more with implacable blue eyes. 'But right now, I need to go to the bathroom. Then I could do with a cup of coffee. It's been a long hard drive.'

When she didn't answer him, or move, Adrian took matters into his own hands, striding off down the hallway in search of the bathroom.

The open doorway on his left revealed a living room, the one on the right a bedroom.

The next door on the right was shut, Adrian presuming this had to be the bathroom. But when he went to open it, Sharni screamed out, 'No!' and came charging down the hallway after him, snatching his hand from the door knob and slamming the door shut again.

'That's not the bathroom,' she said sharply. 'It's in here,' she added, moving along to throw open the next door on the right. 'When you're finished, the kitchen is at the end of the hallway. I'll go make you that coffee.'

Adrian frowned as she hurried off, his curiosity sparked as to what lay behind that other shut door. In a cottage this size, it could only be another bedroom. What could it possibly contain that she didn't want him to see?

He couldn't think of a single thing.

It was probably just a mess, he decided during his visit to the old-fashioned bathroom. The way the outside of the house was a mess.

The kitchen wasn't a mess. It was a large, country-style

room that smelt of recent cleaning. The cupboards were pine, the counter tops painted a dark green. A round table and four chairs sat in the middle of the cork-tiled floor, a wood-burning heater occupying the hearth in one corner. A small flat-screen television—not turned on—sat on top of the surprisingly small fridge. A wide rectangular window stretched over the sink, which looked out over a covered veranda and a tree-covered valley beyond.

Sharni was standing in front of that window with her back to him, her slender shoulders hunched and tense. She turned when she heard him, her eyes angry.

'Why did you have to come?' she snapped. 'Why couldn't you have left me alone?'

'I've already told you why,' he said as he came forward and pulled out a chair at the table.

She shook her head. 'I don't believe you,' she pronounced, then turned to finish making the coffee. 'How do you have your coffee?' she threw over her shoulder. 'I can't remember.'

'Black. No sugar.'

'Aren't you having any?' Adrian asked when she placed the steaming white mug in front of him.

'No,' she said coldly, and crossed her arms again.

'Sit down, then. You make me nervous, standing there like that.'

Her laugh was dry. 'You? Nervous? That'll be the day.'

But she did sit down, opposite him, with the chair pushed well back from the table, her arms still crossed.

'What can I say to make you believe me?' he asked after he'd taken a few sips of the scalding-hot coffee.

'Absolutely nothing. I judge a man by his actions, not his words. You're a confirmed womaniser, Adrian Palmer, and I don't want anything further to do with you. Now, please, drink up your coffee and leave. I have to go out.'

'What for?'

'To buy fresh milk and to collect my dog.'

'Where's your dog?'

'He spent the weekend in a kennel and won't be too happy if I leave him there much longer.'

Adrian was surprised to find that she had a dog. He would have thought she was more a cat person. 'What kind of dog?'

'A Jack Russell terrier.'

'No kidding. I had a Jack Russell terrier when I was a boy. Lovely little dogs, so full of life.'

Sharni sighed. 'Usually. But Mozart hasn't been the same since Ray died. He was Ray's dog, really, not mine.'

Adrian frowned. 'Ray called his dog Mozart?'

'Yes. Why?'

'He's my favourite composer.'

'Mozart is a lot of people's favourite composer. Now, have you finished your coffee?'

Adrian drank it down, then set the empty mug on the table.

'I told you, Sharni, I'm not leaving.'

She stood up and glowered down at him. 'If you don't go, I'll call the police.'

'Don't be ridiculous. Come on,' he said and stood up also. 'I'll go with you whilst you get your dog.'

'You can't!'

'Why not?'

'Because everyone there is going to stare at you.'

'Why?'

'They'll think you're Ray, come back from the dead.'

Adrian frowned. 'I look *that* much like him?'

'Yes.'

'Show me a photo of him, then. Let me see for myself.'

She didn't want to, he could see. Which made Adrian all the more determined. Suddenly, he wanted to know what was behind that shut door, too. He didn't want to leave a stone unturned in the mystery that was Sharni Johnson.

Because nothing she said and did made sense to him. She'd kissed him back at the front door, with a passion that was mind-blowing. So why was she trying to send him away without giving him the slightest chance to prove his sincerity? Even if she wasn't convinced that he cared about her, why not have some more of the great sex they'd shared?

It wasn't logical for a woman to deny herself male company, certainly not one as lonely as Sharni obviously was.

'I can't show you any photos of Ray,' she said stubbornly. 'I packed them all away earlier today.'

'Why would you do that?'

'Because I've decided to sell and move.'

'Good idea.' With a bit of luck he might persuade her to move to Sydney. 'So where are you planning on moving to?'

'That's none of your business.'

'Fine,' he said, whilst privately thinking that he aimed to make it his business. 'I still want to see a photo of Ray. I think I have a right to see exactly how much I resemble him.'

She hesitated for a few seconds, but then seemed to make up her mind. 'Very well,' she said. 'There's one on the piano in the living room which should do. I haven't packed in there yet.'

He followed her down the hallway into the living room, which was a lot chillier than the kitchen. The furniture was country comfort, in warm autumnal colours: a large squashy lounge suite grouped around the unlit hearth, no television set in sight, just several bookcases, crammed with books, along with an upright piano in one corner.

'So who's the piano player?' he asked as he followed her across the room.

'Ray was,' she said.

Adrian frowned. Just another coincidence, he supposed. But he'd always wanted to learn the piano. But his attending an all-boys, mad-about-sport school had stopped him from taking lessons. The few boys there who'd learned the piano had been considered pansies.

'I took that a few weeks before he died,' Sharni said, and nodded towards a silver-framed photo sitting on top of the piano.

Adrian picked up the photo and stared at the man who'd been Sharni's husband.

'Bloody hell,' he muttered under his breath as his shocked gaze studied every feature of the dead man.

'I'm not just like him, am I?' he said, turning to stare at Sharni. 'I could *be* him. Even our hair's the same style!'

'You walk the same as well,' she added for good measure.

For the first time since he'd kissed her at the door, Adrian's confidence over this woman wanting him wavered.

'So *was* it me who made love to you yesterday, Sharni? Or Ray?'

The temptation to lie to him was acute. It would solve all her problems. Or the ones he created in her whirling mind and treacherously weak body.

But something in his voice, and in his eyes, touched her heart.

Adrian was not a man she would have ever thought of as vulnerable. But, suddenly, he was. Maybe it would only be his ego that would be hurt if she lied, but she still could not do it.

'You asked me that yesterday,' she hedged.

'And?'

Her sigh carried reluctance, and resignation. 'I didn't lie to you. I wasn't pretending you were Ray. Not once.'

'How could you *not* be thinking of him? I'm the dead spit of the man, in every way.'

'You might look like Ray, Adrian, but you're two very different people. My husband was…well, he was a very gentle, rather introverted man.'

'Who had a Jack Russell Terrier and played the piano,' Adrian said thoughtfully as he stared down at Ray's photo one more time. 'And read lots of books.'

'Yes.'

He'd gone through a stage a few years ago when he'd read lots of books, becoming quite addicted to legal thrillers. Not so many now. Still…

Adrian walked over to the bookcases to see up close what kind of books his double liked.

The subjects they covered were wide, from romantic sagas to biographies to lots of self-help books. Adrian was thinking he wasn't into that much, when his eyes narrowed on a large book lying flat on one of the bottom shelves. It was entitled *Great Buildings of the World*.

He glanced up at Sharni, who was hovering nearby, looking anxious. 'What did your husband do for a living?'

'He was a draughtsman.'

Adrian's eyebrows rose.

'Yes, I know what you're thinking,' Sharni said. 'Ray told me when we first met that he actually wanted to be an architect.'

'And I always wanted to play the piano.'

They stared at each other for a long time before Adrian shook his head.

'This is crazy. It can't be. I'm not adopted. I know that for a fact. I'm my mother's biological child. There are photos of her pregnant with me in the family album. And photos of me, having my first bath.'

'Could she have had twins? And adopted one out?'

'Mum would never have given away a child. She was a wonderful mother. She always said she would have loved more babies, but something went wrong after I was born and she couldn't have any more.'

'So all these things… They're just coincidences?'

'They must be. They say fact is stranger than fiction.'

'I suppose so,' Sharni murmured. But it was hard to accept. She could see Adrian was finding it hard to accept too, now that he'd seen Ray's photo.

'There are some small differences,' she said. 'In your face. Not from the side so much, but front on. Other people probably wouldn't notice but I did, once we were face to face in that restaurant. You've also got a bigger body frame. And there's…um…something else,' she finished up somewhat awkwardly.

'What?'

'You're circumcised. Ray wasn't.'

Adrian heaved a huge sigh of relief as he placed the photo back on top of the piano. He'd honestly begun to think that his parents had been involved in some ghastly deception.

'That seals it, then. If, by some miracle, Ray and I were twins, we would both have been circumcised at the same time.'

'I guess so,' Sharni said. 'I didn't think of that.'

Adrian smiled. 'Perhaps because you were thinking

of something else at the time you noticed that little detail.'

Adrian took comfort from her blush. How could he have forgotten her delightful responses to him yesterday? There'd been nothing false in them, the extent of her pleasure clearly surprising herself. She'd been a woman discovering true passion for the first time. With him.

Even in hindsight there'd been nothing to indicate that she'd been pretending he was someone else.

Adrian would have liked to pull her into his arms and remind her of the chemistry that had sizzled between them from the moment they'd met. But he wasn't going to risk spoiling what he wanted with Sharni. Which was a real relationship, not just a sexual fling.

'Come on,' he said, and took her hand. 'Let's go get your dog.'

CHAPTER FOURTEEN

HE WAS doing it again, Sharni thought with panic in her heart but excitement fizzing along her veins. Taking over.

'You'll have to stay in the car,' she said as firmly as she could manage. 'I don't want people looking at you and thinking they're seeing a ghost.'

Adrian's sigh sounded exasperated. 'That's ridiculous, Sharni. I'm planning on becoming a fixture in your life, so the sooner your friends get to know what I look like, the better.'

More panic. 'A fixture? What kind of fixture?'

'Friend. Lover. Boyfriend. I'll answer to any of those.'

'Don't I have any say in the matter?'

'You had your say when you kissed me back at the door.'

'After which I asked you to leave.'

His smile was somewhat smug. 'You're the one who said actions speak louder than words. You can tell me to leave till the cows come home but your lips don't lie when they're under mine.'

'You're an arrogant bastard.'

'Who knows what he wants. And that's you, Sharni Johnson.'

His impassioned words made her head swim. So did the look in his eyes.

'Please don't,' she choked out when he lifted her hand to his mouth.

He lowered her hand and nodded, his expression rueful. 'Thank you.'

Sharni blinked. 'For what?'

'For stopping me. I vowed to myself that I would not make love to you today. I was going to show you that my feelings for you encompassed far more than just the physical. But I find being alone with you in this house is a highly corrupting environment. Collecting your dog might be a good thing.'

'Mozart's been known to bite,' Sharni warned. 'Maybe you'd better just leave altogether.'

Adrian smiled at her with his eyes. 'Good bluff, darlin'. Stop thinking up excuses and let's go.'

He was the corrupting environment, she thought as she drove towards the veterinary clinic. No matter where he was.

The man was sex on legs. When he'd kissed her hand back then every pore in her body had begun to dissolve. If his intention was to stay the night—and it seemed unlikely that he would drive back to Sydney at this late hour—then they were sure to end up in bed together, regardless of his so-called resolution not to make love to her today.

The thought of sleeping with Adrian in the same bed that she'd shared with Ray brought waves of guilt.

'You can't stay the night at my place, Adrian,' she said at last.

'I don't intend to. I'm going to book into that motel we just passed. Hey, watch the road!'

Sharni's hands gripped the steering wheel more tightly.

'I won't join you there, if that's what you're thinking.'

'I wasn't.'

That surprised and disappointed her at the same time. Oh, Sharni, Sharni, Sharni, you are a foolish woman.

'So what are you going to do tomorrow?' she asked him.

'Go to work.'

'Oh.' So much for her equally foolish thought that he was going to stay and take her out somewhere. 'The traffic's awfully bad on the highway on a Monday morning,' she advised in flat tones. 'You wouldn't want to get on the road too late.'

'The only road I'll be getting on is the road to Katoomba. I'm going to hit the shops first thing for some suitable clothes, and then I'm coming to your place and I'll start fixing it up.'

When shock sent her eyes jerking away from the road, Adrian grabbed the wheel. 'If you're going to keep driving like that, then I suggest you let me take over.'

Wasn't that what he was already doing?

'You fancy yourself as a handyman, do you?' she said with a touch of irritation. But she suspected the irritation was more with herself than with him. She hated being such a pushover.

He smiled over at her. 'Amongst other things.'

'You are truly incorrigible. But be my guest. The house could do with some work.'

'I did notice.'

His remark wasn't sarcastic, but it still stung.

'I know this will sound pathetic, but I didn't. Notice, that is. Not till I came home yesterday. I think being away opened my eyes to a lot of things.'

'Having a holiday can do that.'

She glanced over at him, surprised by this insightful remark.

'Eyes on the road, madam.'

'It's all right,' she said, turning from the highway into the clinic car park, which was starkly empty at this hour on a Sunday afternoon. 'We're here now.'

'But this is a veterinary hospital,' Adrian said. 'Is your dog sick?'

'No. Though he does come here when he is sick. This is where I work. As a veterinary assistant. Remember? John…That's my boss. He said Mozart could stay here for the weekend. I don't like to leave him with strangers.'

'I see. It looks a nice clean place. But that building's crap. He should have employed a better architect.'

Sharni had to laugh. 'I won't tell John that. Wait here and try to behave yourself.'

He didn't argue with her. Thank heavens. Just rolled

his eyes and stayed put. 'Try not to be too long,' he said. 'Patience is not one of my virtues.'

'You mean you have some?'

He smiled a droll smile. 'What happened to that sweet girl I met yesterday?'

'She found out that her prince charming was really a big bad wolf!' she quipped as she climbed out, slammed the car door and marched off.

John was where he always was on a Sunday afternoon. At the hospital, in the section behind the consultation rooms where he kept his recovering patients. He was an extremely devoted vet and the kindest man Sharni had ever met. Most other vets would have been retired at seventy two, but not John. Healing sick animals was his life.

'Hush up,' she said when she walked in and one of the dogs started barking like a lunatic. 'It's only me.'

John glanced up from where he was tending a large ginger cat.

'Is that Sharni Johnson, actually smiling?'

'Am I?' She hadn't realised. She didn't particularly feel happy, but could not deny that her verbal sparring with Adrian had given her a buzz.

'You certainly are. Looks like that weekend in Sydney has done you the world of good, even if you have come back a day early.'

'I don't know about that. I spent a lot of money on clothes I'll probably never wear.'

'Then maybe it's time you started going places to

wear them,' he advised. 'You're not getting any younger, you know. One day you'll wake up and forty will be just around the corner. Then fifty. Then sixty. Then seventy.'

'Thank you for that cheery advice. How's Mozart been?'

John pulled a face. 'He wouldn't eat. Bess took him into the house and gave him what we were having. That always works with our dogs. But he refused to be tempted. He's out in the back yard, lying under the big pine.'

'Oh, dear! What am I going to do with him, John?'

John shrugged. 'Some dogs are one man dogs and there's nothing you can do about it.'

'I'll take him home and see if I can get him to eat something. Thanks for looking after him.'

'No trouble, love. I'm glad to see that one of you is looking happy. Would you mind if I don't come out with you? I think I should stay with Marmalade.'

'She's not going to die, is she?' That was the one thing Sharni found hard about her job now. Animals dying. Death of any kind could spiral her into a depression within minutes. She no longer watched the news on television for fear of what it might contain.

'Not if I can help it. Off you go now and don't worry too much about Mozart. He'll survive.'

Sharni forced a smile, said goodbye, and left.

But was surviving enough? she wondered as she walked across the back yard towards the big pine. Sometimes surviving was worse than death.

Mozart stood up when she approached, but he didn't

wag his tail, or bark excitedly. Still, he let her pick him up, which was something he didn't let many people do. Any attempt at patting him these days usually brought a snap or a snarl. Louise knew to keep her distance from him. And so did the postman.

It hadn't occurred to Sharni when Adrian came with her that his being in the car would present a problem once they were joined by Mozart. This lack of forethought annoyed her. Because it was typical of her thought processes around Adrian. He made her lose her head.

She also hadn't anticipated Adrian climbing out of the car as she approached with the dog in her arms. She certainly hadn't anticipated Mozart's reaction. He wriggled like mad, burst out of her hold, dropped to the ground then raced to Adrian, going up on his short hind legs and doing three hundred and sixty degree twirls, the way Ray had taught him when he was a little puppy.

'What a clever dog you are,' Adrian said, getting down on his haunches and chucking Mozart under his chin.

Mozart responded by leaping onto his lap, putting his front paws on Adrian's chest, then reaching up to cover Adrian's chin with slurpy licks.

Adrian rose, laughing, and taking Mozart with him. 'And you said he bites, you naughty girl,' he said as he tucked Mozart under one arm. The dog immediately quietened, as if he knew who was the boss once more. But his small dark eyes were alive with happiness, his upwards glances at Adrian the same adoring glances he'd once given Ray.

Sharni swallowed the huge lump in her throat. 'He's not usually like this,' she said. 'Especially with strangers.'

'Maybe he's just glad to be out of there,' Adrian said, nodding towards the clinic. 'Must be like being in jail, being in a kennel. Come on, let's take him home. I'll bet he didn't eat a thing in there all weekend. He feels awfully thin.'

'He hasn't eaten well since Ray died,' Sharni informed him, then added with a frown, 'Or been this happy. I hate to say this, but I…I think he thinks you're Ray.'

Even as she made that statement, Sharni knew it didn't ring true. Dogs didn't recognise people by what they looked like. It was more a matter of scent and voice and mannerisms. You could not fool a dog.

Yet Mozart was obviously fooled. Sharni supposed there was an exception to every rule. Adrian had almost fooled her, for a few seconds. Now, he just made her act foolishly.

'No kidding,' Adrian said, obviously not fazed by the notion. 'Well, I don't mind if you don't mind. Do you mind? What harm is there, if he's happy? You're happy, aren't you, little fella?' he said, and tickled the dog's ribs.

Mozart answered by trying to slobber all over him again.

Adrian laughed. 'See? He's happy. Come on, Mum, get me home, he's telling you. I'm hungry.'

Sharni's stomach contracted at Adrian calling her

Mum, even though she knew he didn't mean anything by it. But it reminded her of the near miss she'd had today when Adrian had almost gone into the nursery. If he was going to work around the house for any length of time, then she would have to tell him about the baby she'd lost. If she didn't, someone else might, like big-mouth Louise from next door.

Better it came from her.

She looked over at him as she climbed in behind the steering wheel. What would he think when she told him? Would he put two and two together and know that that shut door hid a nursery? Would he want to see it?

He wasn't a totally insensitive man. Yesterday, he'd had moments of kindness, and tenderness. He was, however, a bachelor. How could a bachelor understand the grief of losing a child the terrible way she had?

He'd think she was crazy, keeping the nursery as it was all these years. He wouldn't appreciate that it had given her a place to grieve at first. Or that later, she'd been too depressed to follow Janice's suggestion and give everything away to charity.

In truth, she hadn't been in there for ages.

Still, if she was serious about selling and moving—and she was!—then she would have to find the courage to follow her sister's suggestion.

Maybe Adrian would help her do it. With him around, she would have to keep it together. She'd couldn't cry all the time. Or try to hang onto anything.

'You're very quiet,' Adrian said.

Sharni came back to the present, surprised to find that she was almost home. Yet she couldn't even remember starting up the car, let alone the drive back along the highway.

'I was off in another world,' she admitted.

'Thinking good thoughts, I hope.'

'Actually, I was thinking that my next-door neighbour is going to have a fit when she spots you. That car of yours is a gossip magnet, and dear old Louise is a busybody of the first order. She's sure to find an excuse to come over sooner or later. I can only imagine the rain has kept her away so far. That's her house there,' she said as she drove past a small red brick cottage.

'No point in worrying about things you can't control, Sharni. We'll cross the bridge of dear old Louise when we come to it.'

Sharni actually liked that philosophy of life. She'd been brought up in a house where worrying about the future was not the norm. Ray, however, had been a worrier. His adoptive mother had been an anxious, over-protective woman, he'd told her. Not the kind of up-bringing to produce an outgoing, confident man.

'You forgot the milk,' Adrian said as she turned into her driveway.

'It's all right. I can do without. I'll do a proper food shop tomorrow.'

'You're sure? I can go get you some if you like? I know where the garage is. They always have stuff like milk and bread in garages.'

'No, no, Mozart would be most unhappy if you left right now. Come inside and we'll get him something to eat.'

It was a delight to see Mozart gobble up his food for once, but also a worry. What would happen to the dog when Adrian went back to Sydney? Which he would, eventually.

Sharni was under no illusions about Adrian. He found her a challenge at the moment. The fish who'd got away. That was why he was here, she had finally realised. Not *just* for more sex. He was probably telling the truth about that. Because, let's face it, a man like him could get sex anywhere, with more beautiful and much sexier women than herself.

No, he was here to win.

She'd read about personalities like him in some of the many books on the human psyche that Ray had bought in an attempt to work out why he was the way *he* was. She'd read quite a few of them over the last year, trying to heal herself.

'Man, that was one hungry dog,' Adrian said. 'Should I take him out for a walk now? After all, what goes in one end has to come out the other.'

'No need. He has his own special exit,' she said, showing Adrian the one Ray had made in the back door. Immediately, Mozart pushed through the swinging gate and ran out into the back yard. 'He can come and go as he pleases. I do lock it last thing at night, though. To stop the possums getting in.'

'What about bad guys?'

'No, you wouldn't fit.'

Adrian shot her a twisted smile.

'Very funny,' he said. 'So is that how you still think of me? As one of the bad guys?'

'Let's just say the jury's still out,' Sharni retorted.

His eyes were not at all amused. 'If I were really a bad guy, madam, I would already have exploited the one thing you definitely *do* like about me. I could reduce you to begging if I wanted to,' he ground out. 'In fact, you will have to beg me for it, before I touch you again.'

'Never!' she retorted.

His smile was the smile of the devil. 'Never say never, darlin'. You might have to eat your words.'

Sharni's face flamed at the image his words evoked.

So why did just the thought of what Adrian had said bring heat, not just to her cheeks, but to the rest of her body? Why had her mouth gone as dry as the Sahara? Why was her heart racing behind her ribs as if she'd just done a marathon?

His eyes narrowed on hers before he suddenly pushed her away, turned round and strode off towards the hallway.

She wanted to run after him, but she managed not to humiliate herself further.

'I'll be back tomorrow morning,' he called back from the front door. 'Don't forget to keep the home fires burning.'

Sharni groaned at this remark, because of course he

was talking about herself. She was the home fire, burning for him. And she did. Quite literally.

And he knew it.

'Oh, God,' she cried, and sank down into a chair at the kitchen table.

Simultaneous with the sound of Adrian's car roaring off up the street, Mozart shot into the kitchen through his trapdoor. His first action was to glance around the room, then up at her with bright, expectant eyes.

'He's gone, Mozart,' she told the dog.

Mozart dashed off up the hallway. Sharni knew what he was doing. He was checking each room as he'd done so many times during the days after Ray had died.

This time, however, when he came back to the kitchen, he didn't curl up in a corner, whimpering. He jumped up onto the chair that Adrian had occupied and settled down.

He was waiting, Sharni realised. Waiting for his master to return.

Like me, Sharni thought with a telling tightening of her belly.

Would he touch her tomorrow? Kiss her? Make love to her?

No use pretending she didn't want him to any more.

But what if he didn't? What if he made her wait even longer?

She'd die if he did that.

She should have been nicer to him. Shouldn't have called him a bad guy. Even if he was.

Well, not seriously bad. But he was a serial womaniser with no concept of true commitment or caring.

The phone ringing gave Sharni a fright. Who could it be? Maybe Janice. Or John, perhaps?

Before she had time to stand up and answer it, the ringing stopped.

Sharni sighed and sank back into the chair. Probably a wrong number. Still, the phone ringing reminded her that she'd promised to call Janice tonight. When she did, no way was she going to tell her anything about Adrian following her up here. She didn't want her sister to know what was going on. She certainly didn't want to hear all her dire warnings.

Sharni already knew Adrian wasn't in love with her. And, heaven help her, she wasn't in love with him. Love was a warmer, kinder emotion than what was raging through her at this moment. She'd experienced love. With Ray. And this was not love. This was something else entirely. She'd sensed that from the start.

What was consuming her had many names. Sexual attraction; chemistry; desire; passion; lust.

Lust, Sharni decided, came closest to describing what she felt for Adrian.

Lust was one of the seven deadly sins. For good reason, she agonised.

Lust banished your conscience, and your common sense. It made you a slave to your senses, and to your desires, which seemed to become darker and stronger by the moment.

She wanted to go to that motel and throw herself at Adrian's feet. She craved his arms around her and his mouth on hers.

Only her pride stopped her.

But for how long? How long before she begged him to touch her; before she did every wicked thing that was running through her head?

'Oh, God,' she cried, and buried her face in her hands.

CHAPTER FIFTEEN

NEARLY noon, and Adrian still hadn't come.

Sharni was getting agitated. So was Mozart, who was pacing up and down the front veranda. Or he had been, last time she'd looked.

The possibility that Adrian had decided to forget about her and go back to Sydney was a constant torment in her mind. Although to do that seemed terribly cruel. Was Adrian cruel? She hadn't thought so. But what did she know?

He'd said he was going into the shopping centre this morning to buy some work clothes. Sharni had estimated that would probably take him a couple of hours. She'd dashed along to the closest shopping centre to grab some food first thing this morning, leaving herself plenty of time after coming home for some female titivation before Adrian's estimated time of arrival at around eleven.

That ETA had come and gone an hour ago.

For the umpteenth time, Sharni joined Mozart on the front veranda.

The sight of Louise waddling across the street towards her front gate brought a frustrated groan to her lips.

But it was inevitable, she supposed.

'Hello,' Louise called out. 'Nice day, isn't it?'

'Very,' Sharni returned.

'You've been away,' she said, stopping at the front gate when Mozart gave a low growl.

Good dog, Sharni thought.

'Yes. I visited my sister in Swansea,' she lied.

'How nice. I have the most dreadful cold so I won't come too close. I've been in bed all weekend.'

That was good news. Louise's bedroom was at the back of her house, which meant she probably hadn't seen Adrian yesterday, or his car.

But she was going to any second, Sharni thought with a mixture of delight and dismay when she spotted the bright yellow sports car coming down the street.

Louise turned at the sound of the engine, which had a deeper throb than most cars.

'Are you expecting someone?' the older woman asked when Adrian's car did a U-turn at the end of the road and pulled up outside Sharni's house.

Sharni had to think quickly on her feet. 'Yes, I've hired a renovation company to do the place up a bit. I've decided to sell. That's the owner now.'

Sharni was about to add that he looked amazingly like Ray when the words died in her throat.

Because the man who climbed out from behind the wheel didn't look like Ray at all. He didn't look much like Adrian, either. But it *was* Adrian, with very short hair, dark stubble all over his lower face, and a pair of wraparound sunglasses that totally hid his gorgeous blue eyes. He strode round the front of the car, very workmanlike in blue jeans, brown boots, a red checked shirt and a brown bomber jacket, with lambswool trim.

'Mornin, ma'am,' he greeted Louise, who quickly moved out of his way.

'Mornin', Mrs Johnson,' he added with a sneaky wink as he strode up the front path. 'Sorry I'm a bit late. Hi there, little fella,' he directed at Mozart, who quivered with pleasure when Adrian bent to pat him.

'Watch it,' Louise warned. 'He bites.'

'Not me, ma'am. Dogs just love me,' Adrian said as he scooped Mozart up into his arms. 'Now, if you'll excuse us, I need to have a little chat with Mrs Johnson about what needs to be done around here.'

With that, he used his free hand to take Sharni's elbow and shepherd her inside the house, well away from a bug-eyed Louise.

'Did I do well?' he asked once they made it safely into the kitchen.

'You did very well,' she complimented. 'You know, I didn't recognise you when you first got out of the car.'

'Really.' He dropped Mozart gently onto his feet, then swept off his sunglasses and slipped them in his shirt pocket.

Sharni stared up into his ruggedly handsome face, which no longer reminded her so much of Ray. Though his eyes were still the same. 'You look different with your hair like that,' she said. 'And this...' Without thinking, she reached up and ran her hand slowly over his stubbly chin.

Adrian froze under her touch.

Shortly after leaving yesterday, he'd gone through a weak moment when he'd rung Sharni's home number with the intention of apologising for his no-sex-until-she-begged-him threat.

Fortunately, he'd changed his mind before she'd answered. Because he really wanted her to beg him; wanted her to face the depth of her desire for him. *Him*, not her dead husband.

His dramatically changing his appearance this morning had not been done to fool her friends and neighbours. It was a test, one which she seemed to be passing if the look in her eyes was anything to go by.

She still desired him, he realised with a rush of relief.

Unfortunately, he desired her more.

It was agony ignoring the urge to crush her to him. But it had to be done. Because if he gave in and started making love to her, she would never believe that his feelings for her went beyond desire. She would continue to think of him as the big bad wolf; as one of the bad guys.

No. He had to wait. And make her wait, till she couldn't stand waiting any longer. It would be worth it to hear her put her desire into words; to force her to make the first pass.

Adrian replaced his sunglasses, then took a step backwards, so that her hand fell from his face.

'Time for me to get to work,' he said abruptly. 'Where do you keep your lawnmower and garden tools? I'll attack the grounds today. Tomorrow I'll do some general repairs. Then on Wednesday, I'll get started on the painting.'

She frowned up at him. 'Don't you have to get back to your own work in Sydney?'

'No. Like I told you. I'm between projects at the moment.' Not strictly true as of today. He had planned to start on a revolutionary new design for a retirement village, one he was going to enter into a competition, with the winner awarded a multimillion-dollar contract.

But that would just have to go on the backburner for a week or two. His priorities in life had changed.

'The lawnmower and tools?' he repeated with arched brows.

She shrugged, then led him through the back door, down into the back yard where there was a garden shed in the far corner. In there was everything he needed, including a half-full petrol can and a surprisingly wide range of DIY tools, all hanging in a highly organised fashion on a huge board. Adrian liked things to be organised, not being able to stand a messy desk, or messy drawers.

'Can I help?' she asked as he busied himself, filling the mower.

'I'd rather do this by myself,' he replied, not wanting her around him all the time. If he kept her at a distance he just might make it through the day without jumping her very beautiful bones. Adrian was an observant man and it hadn't escaped his notice that Sharni had gone to considerable trouble with her appearance today. Her hair was faultless, falling in smooth bangs around her beautifully made up face. She was only casually dressed, but flatteringly so, in tight black jeans and a cream ribbed jumper that moulded over her breasts and hugged her slender waist. She smelled good, too, her perfume a musky scent, which made him think of sex.

Adrian suspected that subconsciously—or even consciously—she was trying to seduce him.

As he glanced up at her Adrian steeled himself to resist her womanly wiles. 'If you're serious about selling, then there must be things for you to do inside. Give the place a thorough spring-clean, then throw out everything you haven't used or worn in the past two years. That way, when you move, you won't need too big a truck.'

'Yes, yes, I suppose I could do that,' she said in a not very convincing manner.

He straightened and looked hard at her. 'You are serious about selling and moving, aren't you?'

Her arms folded defensively. 'I don't usually say things I don't mean.'

'That's good. You'll have plenty to occupy your mind, then, won't you? Now, if you'll excuse me, I want to get on with this.'

* * *

I *am* serious about selling and moving, Sharni lectured herself as she trailed somewhat reluctantly back inside.

Janice had been over the moon when she'd told her about her decision last night. So there was no going back now, even if inside just the thought of such a massive life change made her feel sick.

She didn't start cleaning, or sorting out her clothes as per Adrian's suggestion. Instead, she stood at the sink, staring through the window, watching Adrian mow the back lawn.

He's even sexier with his hair cut short, she thought.

She liked the stubble on his chin, too.

An erotic image popped into her head of his lying between her naked legs, as he had more than once last Saturday afternoon. She shuddered as she relived the feel of his tongue licking her most sensitive spot. Shuddered a second time as she imagined how it would feel with his roughened cheeks rubbing against the soft flesh of her inner thighs at the same time.

Oh, God. She wanted him to do that to her. Wanted to do it to him as well. Use her mouth on him.

The intensity of her desire was perturbing, but merciless, forcing her to make the most humiliating decision of her life. She would go to him tonight. And she would beg him to take her to bed.

It seemed perverse, Sharni was to think when she called him in for lunch an hour later, that, having come to such a pride-crushing decision, she could behave around him with amazing composure. She coolly served him a very nice lunch, making polite conversation during the fifteen minutes it took him to eat it.

After lunch, she did make a move on cleaning the house, giving the living room a proper going-over, even taking down the curtains and popping them in the washing machine, though she wasn't able to hang them out till Adrian moved from the back yard to the front.

When he refused afternoon tea, saying he wanted to work till the sun went down, Sharni decided to do what Adrian had suggested earlier and go through her wardrobe. It came as no surprise that most of her clothes were over five years old, some of them even older. Lots were hopelessly out of fashion. She quickly filled two garbage bags with things to be given to charity, including several pairs of shoes and a couple of old handbags that had seen better days.

During this rather ruthless throwaway, Sharni kept ignoring the large plastic shopping bag that she'd thrown down in the bottom of her wardrobe after returning from Sydney on Saturday. It contained the outfit she'd worn to *The Phantom* and which she'd never wanted to look at ever again.

Even now, she remained hesitant, till, in a burst of self-irritation, she grabbed the shopping bag and spilled its contents onto the bed.

The beaded top sparkled up at her, its neckline not as low cut as she'd thought. Sharni picked up the skirt, pleased to see that it hadn't creased one bit. She laid out the whole outfit on top of the patchwork quilt, placing the shoes on the floor under the hem of the skirt.

It didn't look anything special like that. It needed a woman's body in it.

Her heartbeat quickened as she quickly stripped off down to her panties and pulled the clothes on before she could think better of it. She didn't bother with pantihose this time. After all, she wasn't going anywhere. She just wanted to see what she'd looked like last Saturday night.

The shoes took her a while, her fingers clumsy with the bows at her ankles. Finally, she stood up, astonished at the height of the heels and how sexy they made her feel.

It only took her five steps to cross the bedroom to where there was a cheval mirror in one corner. But they were enough to transform her once again into the turned-on creature who'd let Adrian have sex with her bending over a chair.

Sharni stared when she saw her reflection. Who was that girl with the wide dilated eyes and the panting parted lips?

'Going somewhere?'

She whirled at Adrian's voice, embarrassment making her face flame. 'How dare you sneak up on me like that?'

'I didn't sneak. I knocked on the back door to tell you that I'd finished for the day, but you didn't answer. It still looks great on you, by the way. But not exactly the right outfit for cleaning. Unless, of course, you've something else in mind…'

He levered himself away from where he'd been leaning on the doorframe, his blue eyes glittering as they raked over her.

She didn't say a word. Couldn't. Till he took a step into the room.

'Don't come in here!' she cried out.

He halted, his eyes clouding over with frustration. 'Why not? You want me to. You know you do.'

'Not in here,' she choked out.

His eyes narrowed as he glanced around the room. 'Oh, I see. Not in here, in Ray's bedroom. Or in Ray's house. Very well. I'll try to be sensitive to your feelings, though for pity's sake the man's been dead for five years. Somehow I don't think he would mind.'

'*I'd* mind!'

'Very well. Come to my motel room. Tonight. At ten.'

'*That* late?' The moment those two telling words left her mouth Sharni knew there was no going back.

'Take it or leave it,' he bit out. 'It's room eighteen. The place isn't full so there's plenty of parking spaces nearby.'

She hated him at that moment. Hated him and wanted him at the same time. So much for her earlier composure. Her pride was once again in tatters, lust reigning supreme with all its primal power.

'I will take your silence for agreement.'

She gritted her teeth and glowered at him.

'By the way, don't wear that,' he snapped. 'That's far too many clothes for what I have in mind. The shoes can stay, but nothing else. Absolutely nothing else.'

Shock sent her mouth gaping wide. 'I can't come to your door, stark naked!'

'Then wear a coat. But I want you totally naked underneath.'

'That's disgusting.'

'No. That's what you'll have to do to get what you want. I am what you want, aren't I, Sharni? Or is just sex with any man now? Tell me so that I can be sure of where I stand.'

'You *are* cruel,' she threw at him.

'A cruel man would not have stopped at this door,' he refuted. 'Now tell me what I want to hear, Sharni. Or. God help me, I'm going to go get in my car and I'm never coming back.'

For a split second, she almost let him go. But the devil wouldn't allow it. He whispered in her ear, promising wicked pleasures that only Adrian could give her. All for the price of a few simple words.

'I don't want sex with any other man,' she blurted out. 'Only you.'

'And you'll do what I asked?'

'Yes,' she said, trembling at the thought.

'Don't be late,' he growled. And was gone.

CHAPTER SIXTEEN

ADRIAN found the next five hours almost unbearable. He managed to force some dinner down. And he drank way too much, searching for some mental peace.

But nothing could ease the emotional torment that had consumed him back in that bedroom, once he'd realised that Sharni would never love him. Because she was still in love with her husband.

The pain of this pride-shattering discovery had made him cruel, as she'd said.

But she was cruel, too.

Agreeing to his outrageous demands had shown him better than any words that she didn't want his love, or his caring. Just his body.

Adrian had no doubt that she would show up right on time, wearing nothing but her birthday suit and those shag-me shoes. And when she did, there would be nothing left for him but to do exactly that, till she begged him to stop.

* * *

Sharni could not believe that she was doing this. Driving to a motel for an assignation with Adrian with nothing on but a trench-coat and a pair of high heels.

What would happen if she had a car accident? What would the ambulance officers think?

That you're a whore, came back the soul-destroying answer.

So why didn't her soul feel destroyed? Why were her only feelings those of anticipation and excitement?

Maybe I've sold my soul to the devil. Maybe I'm possessed.

The sight of the motel sign on the right sent her stomach into uncontrollable flutters. Nearly there.

'You can still drive past,' she urged herself out loud. 'Still go home.'

She didn't do either. She turned the car into the motel's concrete driveway, her heart pounding behind her ribs.

The drive past Reception brought another burst of anxiety that someone might stop the car and ask her what she was doing here. No one did, but by the time she parked next to Adrian's yellow car Sharni felt faint with nervous tension.

No one else was arriving or leaving, she noted with relief as she climbed out of her car, closed the door, then locked it.

'Oh, Lord,' she said with a shaky sigh, then turned and made her way very unsteadily to the door of unit number eighteen, which was thankfully on the ground floor of the two storeyed building.

Scooping in a deep breath, Sharni gripped her car keys with one hand whilst she knocked with the other.

No answer.

She knocked again.

Still no answer.

Her head whirled when it occurred to her that Adrian might not be going to answer.

Suddenly, the door was wrenched open and there he stood, dripping wet with a white towel slung low around his hips.

'Sorry,' he muttered, lifting his hand to sweep back hair that was no longer there. 'I was in the shower, and didn't hear you knock.'

'You…you said ten o'clock.'

'I lost track of time.'

She blinked. How could he have lost track of time? She'd been counting down every second, dying for the moment when they would be together again.

'I'm sorry too,' she choked out. 'Look, I don't think I can do this, Adrian. Not now…'

'What in hell are you talking about?'

'Your asking me to come here dressed like this was some kind of payback, wasn't it? You wanted to humiliate me. You don't care about me at all. Not really.'

His face filled with too many mixed emotions for her to fathom.

He shook his head, his arms rising and falling from his sides in an attitude of total exasperation. 'Hell, Sharni, I'm just a man, not a saint. Yes, I confess there was an element of revenge in my demands. But that was because I thought *you* didn't care.'

'Oh…'

Did she care about him?

Sharni wasn't sure. All she could be sure of was that the sight of him standing there in nothing but a towel made her heart race and her insides go to mush. All she could think about was his being inside her again.

Maybe she was a whore after all. Or she was, with him.

'For pity's sake, don't just stand there, looking guilty,' he ground out, pulling her into the room and shutting the door behind her. 'Like I told you last Saturday, there's nothing wrong with enjoying yourself in the sack. It also isn't mandatory that you fall in love with every lover you have in your life. But it would be nice not to be thought of as just a piece of meat.'

'But I don't think that!'

'Don't you?'

'No!'

'Then how do you think of me? Be honest now.'

'I'm not sure what I think, or feel. You've confused me from the start.'

'Because I look like Ray. No, don't bother to keep denying it. It's written all over your face. At least I know where I stand now, and I won't go imagining tonight means more than it means. Now take that damn coat off and let me look at you.'

She stared at him, astonished at how such an angrily delivered request could turn her on with all the speed and power of a lightning bolt. Her nipples tightened against the silk lining of the coat, her stomach flipping over in anticipation of what was to come.

'Don't make me take it off you,' he went on, his blue eyes glittering.

Her hands trembled as they lifted to the top button, her head dizzy with instant desire. Suddenly, she could not wait to stand naked before him. To have those cold, sexy eyes on her.

She'd taken ages earlier this evening preparing herself for this moment. She'd bathed at length, she'd rubbed scented moisturiser into her denuded skin, then painted her nails a deep scarlet, her mouth glossed to match.

And now she was about to show him all that she had done.

The coat dropped off her shoulders and she stood there, frozen.

'You shouldn't have, you know,' he muttered as his heavy-lidded gaze raked over her. 'I won't have any mercy on you now. But then you haven't come here for mercy, have you?' he said as he stripped off the towel and walked slowly towards her.

Sharni's mouth dropped open at the sight of him. He was so huge, and so hard.

She swallowed. Then swallowed again.

He smiled the devil's smile, then pulled her roughly to him.

'I'm not going to kiss you,' he grated out when she turned her face expectantly up to his. 'Not this first time.'

Sharni gasped when he took her up into his arms and literally threw her on the bed. His hands were brutal as they pried her legs wide apart, his penetration just as savage. Her raw groan echoed the mad mixture of pleasure and pain that ricocheted through her as he grabbed her hips and drove in even deeper.

The swiftness of his orgasm shocked Sharni, her strangled cry of protest bringing a wry laugh to his lips.

'Looks like I won,' he said.

'You really are a bastard,' she returned with a flash of true venom.

He levered himself up onto his elbows, then smiled down at her. 'And you, my love, are beautiful beyond compare.'

Sharni groaned. Why, oh, why, did he have to throw in that kind of compliment when she wanted to hate him?

'I think a hot shower is in order,' he said. 'Then back to bed for some serious sex.'

Adrian lay stretched out on the bed next to her, his hands behind his head, his eyes on the ceiling. Sharni was sleeping, her back to him, her breathing deep and even, the sleep of a thoroughly satisfied woman.

For a man who'd had several whiskeys before she'd arrived, he'd acquitted himself extremely well. Never before had he made love to a woman so many times in succession.

What on earth were you trying to prove, Adrian? he asked himself. That you're the greatest lover in the world? Do you honestly think giving her multiple orgasms would make her fall in love with you?

Adrian sighed and turned his head towards the bedside clock, the red numbers showing one seventeen.

He should try to sleep, he supposed. But sleep didn't seem important any more. He had to find a way to win this woman's heart.

It wasn't going to be through sex, he finally accepted. And it probably wasn't going to be because he helped her fix up her house.

There was something about him that didn't fulfil her. Something that her husband had, and that he obviously didn't.

Adrian wasn't used to not getting what he wanted in life. Wasn't used to being considered second best.

This time, however, things seemed to be out of his control.

Felicity would be pleased to know, he realised with considerable irony, that she would probably get her wish.

A woman was going to break his heart.

And her name was Sharni Johnson.

CHAPTER SEVENTEEN

'So what's this I hear about some handsome hunk doing up your place?'

Sharni's head shot up from where she was helping John operate on a kelpie who'd had a run-in with a car.

'How on earth…?'

'Louise came in yesterday with her cat for me to worm,' John explained, without lifting his head from what he was doing.

An exasperated sigh punched through Sharni's lips. 'That woman!'

Her Nosy Parker neighbour had taken every opportunity during the last few days to drop over. Unfortunately, Mozart had stopped snapping and snarling at her, Adrian's presence having changed the dog's personality back into the engaging little terrier he'd been when Ray had been alive.

'That's not an answer to my question,' John pointed out. 'Which is?'

'Who is this hunk and where does he come from?

He's not a local because I also heard he's staying at the motel down the road. Been there all week.'

Sharni's mouth dropped open. 'How on earth do you know *that*?'

'When a man drives a bright yellow Corvette, he's going to be noticed.'

At last John raised his head, having completed the stitches.

'So tell me about him.'

Sharni couldn't possibly tell him the truth. She'd be way too embarrassed, especially how she'd spent every evening this week.

'He's just a friend of a friend from Sydney,' she said. 'He's helping me do up the house with a view to selling.'

'A friend of a friend? Don't take me for a fool, Sharni. He's more than that.'

'Very well…yes,' she admitted, blushing. 'Yes, he is.'

'That's good, then. It's high time you started to live again. And it's good that you've decided to sell. That place has far too many bad memories for you. So tell me a bit more about him?' he finished up, his eyes dropping back to his patient.

Sharni hesitated, then decided it might be a relief to talk to someone who was both sympathetic and objective. She'd been tempted a couple of times to ring Janice and tell her about her ongoing affair with Adrian, but was worried about her sister's reaction.

She still wasn't about to confess all to John. There

were some details that would simply have to remain her own dark little secret.

'He *is* a friend of a friend, actually,' she said, hoping this made the speed of her affair not seem so sluttish. 'I…um…I ran into him when I was down in Sydney last weekend.'

'What does he do for a living? Something tells me he's not a house painter, not driving a car like that.'

'He's an architect. A very good one.'

'Mmm. He'd be quite a catch, then.'

'I have no intention of ever marrying him!' This was the kind of comment she would have expected from Janice.

John glanced up again. 'Why not? The man must be mad about you to spend every day working like a dog out in this weather.'

It had been bitterly cold all week, with today just a little bit warmer.

It bothered her somewhat, the thought that Adrian might be in love with her. She didn't want him to be in love with her.

'I've only known him a week,' she said.

'I only knew my Bess for two days before I decided to marry her.'

'Adrian's not into marriage.'

'What's he into, then?'

Sharni was glad John's eyes were on the dog and not her reddening cheeks.

'Brunettes,' she said a bit sharply.

John looked up and laughed. 'Sydney is full of brunettes, love. He doesn't have to come to Katoomba to find one.'

'I think I was the one who got away.'

'Ah. I see. You became a challenge.'

Not as much as she would have liked to be, she thought as she recalled the way she'd presented herself to him last Monday night.

Adrian seemed to like making her do things that were potentially humiliating. He'd vowed to make her beg. And she had, this past week, more than once. She'd done a lot of other things, too.

Thank God she was at work today and didn't have to endure the frustration of being around the house, watching him and wanting him.

He never touched her there. Or kissed her. But he would look at her occasionally and she would literally burn for him. It was no wonder that by the time each evening came she was beyond shame. Beyond everything but doing whatever he wanted her to do.

'What are you afraid of with this man, Sharni?'

John's question startled her.

'Ray wouldn't mind, you know,' he went on before she could answer. 'He would want you to be happy. If this man loves you, then give him a chance.'

She shook her head. 'You don't understand.'

'I understand more than you think. You're different this week, Sharni. You've come to life again. Now all you have to do is decide to love again.'

'Love is not a decision, John. It just happens.'

'Then let it happen. Don't shut this man out. I'll bet you haven't told him about the baby you lost, have you?'

Sharni stiffened. 'No.'

'Then you should.'

But she didn't want to. Didn't want to do or say anything that would prevent her going to his motel room tonight.

She knew what she was living was just a fantasy. Knew it would end one day. But she wasn't going to end it. That would have to come from Adrian.

Till then...

'How's Mozart?' John asked, obviously changing the subject.

'He's fine.'

'Louise said he's a changed dog since your helper arrived.'

Sharni gritted her teeth. Louise again! But she refused to bite. Pity Mozart had given up the habit. 'He does seem to be enjoying having a man around the house.'

'Dogs are sensitive creatures. Maybe he knows something that you don't know.'

'Like what?'

John shrugged. 'Who knows? If I was Dr Dolittle, I could ask Mozart for you.'

Sharni was late leaving the clinic that Friday afternoon, an emergency coming in at the last moment. She usually knocked off at four, but by the time she arrived home her watch showed after five, and the sun had just set.

Adrian, however, was still painting the newly mended front fence with the paint spray-gun he'd hired the previous day. Mozart was keeping a safe distance from the spray, running to greet Sharni when she arrived.

'What you know,' she told the dog as she bent to stroke his head, 'is where you're best off.'

Adrian lifted the protective glasses from his paint-spattered face at that moment, and smiled over at her. 'Just five more minutes and it'll be done. What do you think?'

She gazed with true admiration at all he'd achieved in five short days. John was right. He had worked like a mad dog, especially today. When she'd left this morning, the house had only been half painted. Now it shone a brilliant white under the fading light.

'It looks great,' she said. 'But you must be exhausted.'

His smile turned wicked. 'Not that exhausted. But I'll need some time to clean up and get a few things ready before you come.'

Sharni froze. 'What kind of things?' she asked, unable to keep the worry out of her voice.

Last night, he'd introduced her to some mild bondage, securing her wrists behind her back with the sash of his bathrobe, telling her to pretend that she was a love-slave who'd been sold to an evil prince who could do what he liked to her. He, of course, was the evil prince. He'd turned her on with the erotic verbal pictures he painted of her being kept naked for his pleasure; of being shackled to his bed every night; of being made to kneel before him on command, and take him into her mouth.

Which she had.

But she didn't want things to go any further than that.

Worry crinkled her forehead.

'Not those kind of things,' he told her brusquely. 'Shall we say eight? No, that's a bit early. Make it eight-thirty.'

Eight-thirty! That was eons away. Last night it had been seven-thirty.

'Wear what you wore when I first saw you in Sydney,' he commanded, then returned to doing what he was doing.

She just stared at him, her heart thudding behind her ribs. But he didn't look up at her again. He wouldn't, she knew. This was what he always did at the end of each day. Gave his orders for the evening ahead, then ignored her.

It always turned her on. Always. But more so, each time.

Shaken, she let herself into the house and ran to her bedroom where she threw herself onto the bed and burst into tears. What she was crying about she had no idea. This was what she wanted with Adrian, wasn't it? A strictly sexual affair.

Yes, of course it was, she told herself, and began punching the pillows. I don't want to love him. Or for him to love me. I don't!

But the tears kept coming and so, finally, did acceptance of the hidden truth.

John had been so right. She *was* afraid. Afraid of

giving her heart and having it broken once more. Afraid of loving and losing.

But what she was doing with Adrian no longer made her feel good about herself. If she kept going, she would end up turning into a conscienceless sex-addict.

It had to stop. And it had to stop tonight!

CHAPTER EIGHTEEN

SHARNI had worked herself up into a right state by the time she arrived at Adrian's motel-room door that night.

It wasn't going to be easy, telling him that she didn't want to do this any more; that she wanted a real relationship.

She should not have worn the clothes he'd commanded her to wear, she realised as she lifted her hand to knock. It didn't set the right tone. She should have come in old jeans and the most unattractive jumper she owned. Or a daggy track-suit. She certainly should not have taken so much time over her hair and make-up. She very definitely should have put on a bra under her pink jumper.

Erect nipples poking out were going to give him the wrong message.

'Oh!' she exclaimed when Adrian swept open the door. Not because he was naked, as he had been the previous night. But because the room was filled with candles of varying shapes and sizes, all lit and glowing in the darkness.

'You like?' He smiled as he took her hand and drew her inside.

'It's…lovely.'

'I thought I'd do romance tonight, complete with champagne.'

He shut the door, then walked over to the coffee-table where there was an ice bucket hiding in the middle of the candles, along with two tall wineglasses. Some soft music was playing in the background, probably from the radio.

Sharni watched, torn, whilst he popped the cork and filled the glasses. How could she tell him that she didn't want to do *this*? This was sweet and, yes, romantic. Nothing like their erotically charged rendezvous last night. *He* was different too. He was dressed, for starters, in stylish grey trousers and an open-necked royal blue silk shirt. He looked very handsome and elegant. He'd shaved as well, she noticed.

'When on earth did you find time to do all this?'

'Yours is not to reason why, beautiful. And you certainly are that tonight,' he added as he handed her a glass.

'Thank you,' she said, struggling with the temptation not to say anything now.

He eyed her closely when she didn't drink. 'Is there something wrong? Have I made a mistake with the candles and champagne?'

'No, no, I love them. It's just…'

'Just what?'

'Nothing,' she said, and took a quick swallow of the champagne. 'Nothing.'

Adrian gripped his glass so hard he was surprised it didn't snap.

Nothing was going to work with this woman.

It was perfectly obvious she was disappointed. She didn't want romance. She wanted sex. Rough sex, loveless sex.

She liked him talking dirty to her. Liked being tied up and ravaged. Liked playing at being his love-slave.

He'd mistakenly thought that she'd get bored with nothing but sex. That she'd eventually want something more.

He'd been a fool!

Tonight would definitely be his swansong. The house was in pretty good order. She could sell it now without losing too much money. As for him…he was out of here. Or he would be in the morning.

Tonight, however, was going to be just for him. He was going to have her every which way, without giving a hoot if she enjoyed it or not!

His cell phone ringing snapped him out of his increasingly vengeful thoughts.

'Excuse me,' he said abruptly, and moved over to where he'd put his phone on the bedside table.

'Adrian Palmer,' he answered.

'Adrian. It's your mother.'

'Mum! It's not like you to ring me on my mobile.'

'I did try to ring you at your home number but I keep getting your answering machine. I've left several messages for you to ring me back, but you haven't.'

'Sorry. I'm away at the moment.'

'Not on holidays, surely. You never go on holidays. Or visit your mother,' she added snippily.

He had to smile. 'You're right again, Mum. I've been working. So what's up?'

'Does something have to be up for me to ring you?'

Not really. She rang him on a regular basis. But it seemed she'd been pretty desperate to contact him this time.

'I wanted to see if you'd like to fly up and visit me this weekend.'

'Is there any particular reason?'

'Just that I haven't seen you since Easter. Of course, if you're working…'

'I'd love to come,' he said immediately.

'That's wonderful. When can I expect you?'

'Just one sec.'

He put the phone on temporary hold and looked straight at Sharni, thinking this was sure to be the final nail in the coffin of his non-relationship with her.

'My mother has asked me to fly up this weekend for a visit,' he said. 'Would you like to come with me?'

Her eager smile was so unexpected that he nearly dropped the phone. 'I'd love to,' she said. 'But…'

'But what?'

'What about Mozart?'

'We'll take him with us.'

'Could we?'

'Why not?'

'He doesn't settle too well in strange places. I tell you what. We could take him to my sister's place at Swansea, then fly the rest of the way from Newcastle airport.'

'Or we could drive,' he counter suggested. 'We could stop at a motel midway tomorrow night, then go the rest of the way on Sunday morning.'

She seemed pleased with that idea. 'I'd like that. I'm not all that keen on flying.'

Adrian's elation came through in his voice as he reconnected with his mother. 'Mum, would you mind if I brought someone with me?'

'What, you mean a girl?' No missing the shock in his mother's voice.

'Yes.'

'I can't believe it. Are you serious?'

'Yes,' he said, and glanced over at Sharni. 'Very.'

'I was beginning to think you might be gay.'

Adrian had to laugh. 'Sorry. No such luck.'

'Oh, Adrian, I'm so pleased.'

'Wait till you meet her. Look, I'm going to drive up, so we won't get to your place till lunch-time on the Sunday. Of course, I won't come unless you cook my favourite dinner,' he added teasingly.

'Baked leg of lamb.'

'Right in one.'

His mother chuckled. 'You always did love your baked lamb.'

'With apple pie and ice cream for afters.'

'I'm glad to see you're still a simple boy at heart. So what's she called, this girl?' his mother asked.

'Sharni,' he said, and looked over at her with adoring eyes.

Sharni felt the impact of his loving glance right down to her toes.

Never before had Adrian looked at her that way. It shattered any lingering doubt that he might only have wanted her for sex, making her feel both wonderful and ashamed at the same time.

She didn't catch the rest of his conversation with his mother, already planning in her mind what she would say to him when he came off the phone.

He turned to her after hanging up, his expression somewhat guarded. 'I have to admit you've surprised me,' he said. 'I was sure you'd say no.'

Her smile was soft. 'I might have, even as recently as yesterday. But I realised today that I was acting like a fool. I'm sorry I've let you think that all I wanted from you was sex, Adrian. That's not true. I want more than just an affair with you.'

'How much more?'

'I don't know yet. But I'd like the opportunity to find out.'

He frowned at her. 'Does that mean you don't want any sex tonight?'

She looked at him, at the candles, at the bed.

To lie didn't seem the best way to begin a relationship.

'I don't want sex. No.'

He could not hide his disappointment.

'I want you to make love to me,' she added, and walked into his waiting arms.

CHAPTER NINETEEN

'I'M STILL totally gobsmacked,' Janice said, shaking her head as she glanced over at Sharni.

The two sisters were sitting under the covered pergola at the back of Janice's house. Pete was busy cooking steak and sausages on the nearby barbecue whilst Adrian stood next to him with a light beer in his hands. Janice's two boys were haring around the back yard, playing army games, with Mozart chasing after them, having the time of his life.

'You mean about how much Adrian looks like Ray?' Sharni returned.

'Well, yes, that too. It's no wonder you thought he could have been Ray's twin brother. But I was thinking more of the change in you. You're positively glowing.'

Sharni smiled. 'I'm very happy,' she said.

Last night had been wonderful, Adrian showing her he could be a tender as well as a dominating lover. Then today, during the car ride here, they'd finally started talking in a deep and meaningful way. She knew all about his childhood, which sounded pretty perfect. His parents had obviously doted on him.

Adrian knew a lot more about her background, too, including the tragic death of her mother when Sharni had been only thirteen, plus her poor father's succumbing to alcoholism afterwards, resulting in his death from liver failure a few years back.

One thing he still didn't yet know, however, was about the baby she'd lost. She couldn't seem to find the right moment to bring the subject up.

'He loves you,' her sister pronounced.

'Yes,' Sharni agreed, despite his never having said so much in words.

But she had seen his love last night. And felt it, over and over.

Janice frowned. 'Don't you love him back, Sharni?'

'I do,' she said. 'He's a wonderful man, and a marvellous lover.'

'But?' her sister prompted.

Sharni sighed. Trust Janice to pick up on the one lingering doubt she had about her own feelings. 'It doesn't feel the same as what I had with Ray. Don't get me wrong. It's great, what we have together. But there's something missing.'

Janice said nothing for a minute or two, just sat there, with a thoughtful expression on her face. 'I know what's missing,' she said at last.

'What?'

'Need.'

'What do you mean? Need?'

'Sharni, as a kid, you were always bringing home stray cats and birds with broken wings. You loved looking after wounded animals. That was what Ray was, another wounded animal. His needy nature fulfilled your nurturing nature. I'll bet that, down deep, you don't think Adrian needs you. You believe he'd survive without you.'

'Well, he would. Just look at him, Janice. He has everything a man could have. Looks, brains, success, charm, confidence. He could get any woman he wants.'

'But he only wants *you*, dear sister. Can't you see that?'

She could. And she still wasn't sure why.

'Have you told him about the baby?' Janice asked gently.

'Not yet,' she admitted. 'But I will. Soon.'

Sharni could feel her sister frowning at her.

'I've only known him a week, Janice,' she said swiftly. Although it had felt like a lifetime.

'Don't let him get away, Sharni.'

Sharni was still thinking about her sister's words of advice when they resumed their trip North shortly after two.

'I've booked us into a motel at Nambucca Heads,' Adrian told her as the powerful car began to eat up the miles along the Pacific Highway. 'That's a bit more than halfway to our destination.'

'Great,' she said, and settled right back into the leather seat.

Adrian slanted her a warm smile. 'Comfy?'

Sharni's smile carried appreciation. 'This is a gorgeous car to ride in. So smooth.'

'Like they say in the classics, you only get what you pay for.'

'Mmm.'

'Mozart didn't seem to mind our leaving him behind,' he remarked.

'He's a different dog since you came along. Doesn't even snap at Louise any more. Which is a shame,' Sharni added drily.

Adrian laughed. 'She's not that bad.'

'You don't have to live next to her.'

'True. Care for some music? Or do you want to talk some more?'

Now was her chance to tell him about the baby. But once again, she shied away from the subject.

'Some music would be nice,' she said. 'Janice talked non-stop and I'm feeling a little tired.'

'Why don't you try to have a nap?'

Adrian turned on the radio and she closed her eyes.

Sleep came surprisingly quickly, possibly because she hadn't had much rest during the past week, or possibly because she'd had a couple of glasses of red wine with her barbecue lunch.

When Sharni resurfaced, she was startled to find that the sun had set and they were turning off the main highway.

'Feeling refreshed, Sleeping Beauty?' Adrian asked.

'Much. Where are we?'

'Nearly there.'

'You must be tired of driving.'

'A little. We might eat in tonight. Would Chinese do?'

'Sounds good to me.'

'Do you know you are the most accommodating woman?'

'I come from a long line of accommodating women.'

Adrian laughed. 'You could be right. Your sister's great. And so is her husband. I won't mind having them for in-laws.'

Sharni sucked in sharply. 'What did you say?'

'You heard me.'

'Are you asking me to marry you?' Sharni could not keep the shock from her voice.

'Damn. I meant to do it right, down on one knee with a huge diamond in my hand. And so I will. When I get the chance.'

'But…but…you haven't even said that you love me.'

'Really? I thought I did. Last night.'

'No, you didn't.'

'Damn. Another boo boo.' He pulled over to the side of the road, skidding a little in some gravel before stopping abruptly and turning to face her.

'Then let me remedy that mistake immediately,' he said, cupping her face and kissing her startled lips. 'I love you, Sharni Johnson. I love you so much that I refuse to live the rest of my life without you as my wife.'

'Marriage is a big step, Adrian.'

'Yes, I know.'

'But I...I might not be able to have...um...children.' She'd almost said *more* children.

'We'll cross that bridge when we come to it. Together.'

That touched her. Terribly.

But he was also doing it again. Taking over. Much too fast this time.

'You're rushing me,' she said.

'Life is short, Sharni.'

'I need more time.'

'Not too long. I'm not a patient man.'

Her smile was wry. 'I've gathered that.'

'But you do love me, don't you?' he said, kissing her again. More hungrily this time.

By the time his mouth lifted, her head was swimming and her heart was pounding.

'Yes,' she said. 'Yes, I love you.'

He smiled the smile of a satisfied man.

Adrian was smiling that same smile into the bathroom mirror the following morning when Sharni came in to tell him their breakfast had arrived.

She'd become used to the small differences between him and Ray—especially around his face. So the unexpected sight of Ray's features looking back at her from that mirror shocked Sharni rigid.

But then he turned around and she thought she must be going mad. Because face to face, the differences were all there again.

'What's wrong?' he said.

'What? Oh, nothing. Nothing. Breakfast's ready.'

'Good, because we have to be on the road soon if we're going to make it to Mum's place by lunch-time.'

His mother lived at Kingscliff, a seaside town not far south of the border between New South Wales and Queensland. They reached it just before noon, Sharni tensing a little at the prospect of meeting Adrian's mum. But she tried not to show it.

Kingscliff was a truly lovely spot, the beach long and white and inviting. His mother's house was lovely too, a long, two-storeyed blond-brick place, perched on the top of a hill, perfectly positioned for a splendid view of the Pacific Ocean. Distance-wise, it was probably only two hundred metres to the beach, and even less to the main road, which had plenty of shops and restaurants.

'This used to be our holiday house,' Adrian explained as they climbed out of the car. 'Dad's practice was in Brisbane, but we spent every Easter and Christmas down here. When he retired, he told me he wanted to live here, permanently. But the house was only half the size then. He asked me to draw up some plans for a more substantial but traditional home, and, voilà, you have what you see today.'

'You are obviously a brilliant architect,' Sharni said, and was being given an affectionate hug when the front door opened and a lady who looked nothing like Adrian emerged.

She was very short, with silvery grey hair, dark brown eyes and a large nose, which he hadn't inherited.

Her rather plain face broke into a wide smile as she hurried down the sloping path.

'You're earlier than I expected,' she said. 'I hope you didn't speed, you bad boy.'

Adrian laughed, and gave her a big hug. 'I tried, but Sharni told me she'd have my guts for garters.'

'Good girl,' Adrian's mother said warmly. 'He needs reining in, my boy. He think he's invulnerable.'

Sharni smiled. 'Yes, I have noticed that.'

'I can imagine,' his mother said drily, then came forward to give Sharni a hug as well. 'You've no idea how glad I am to meet you, my dear. Do you realise you are the first girl that Adrian has brought home since high school?'

'I'm hardly a girl, Mrs Palmer. I'm thirty.'

'You look like a girl to me. I'm seventy-six next birthday.'

'You don't look it.'

'Oh, she's a sweetie, this one,' she said, linking her arms with Sharni. 'You can keep her, Adrian.'

'I intend to,' he said, shooting Sharni a possessive glance.

'By the way, call me May,' his mother said as she drew her up the steep driveway to the open front door.

The knot in her stomach finally unravelled, Sharni's tension soothed by the genuine warmth of the woman's welcome. It had worried her that Adrian's mother might think she wasn't good enough for her brilliant son.

The house was as well designed inside as outside, with the garages and guest and rumpus rooms downstairs and the master bedroom and living areas upstairs. It was furnished the way Sharni would have expected a seventy-six-year-old lady to furnish her home, with an eye to stylish comfort rather than any particular fashion.

She liked the furniture a lot, especially the pale-green-velvet-covered lounge suite with its huge armchairs and large squashy cushions.

After a brief visit to the bathroom, Sharni allowed herself to be settled on the lounge with a cream sherry served in a beautiful crystal glass. The smell of baking lamb permeated the air, whetting her appetite and making her feel even more at home.

'So what do you think of Mum?' Adrian whispered when his mother retreated to the kitchen to check on the progress of the meat.

Sharni didn't think she should say that his mother was nothing like him at all, except perhaps for her charm.

'She's very nice,' she said.

The woman herself bustled back into the lounge room and swept up her own sherry from one of the many side tables dotted around the room. 'Dinner won't be ready for another forty minutes,' she said as she sat down. 'Are you sure you won't have a drink, Adrian? There's some beer in the fridge, if you'd prefer.'

'I'll have some wine with dinner. Meanwhile, there's something I want to show Sharni.'

He stood up and moved across the room to a long oak sideboard, which had more framed photos sitting on it than Sharni had ever seen. Most of them were of Adrian, but some were of his parents. Even from a distance, Sharni could see that his father had been only marginally taller than his mother. So where had Adrian got his height from?

'Are the family photo albums still in here?' Adrian asked as he slid open one of the lower doors.

'Yes,' his mother replied. A little tensely, Sharni thought.

All those niggling doubts she'd had about Adrian's parentage came back with a rush, twisting her stomach back into a tight knot.

'Ah… Here's the one I want,' Adrian said.

'This entire album is devoted to yours truly,' he added after he sat back down next to her and opened the album across both their laps. 'There's Mum when she was preggers. About six months, weren't you, Mum?'

'About that,' his mother replied tautly.

The photo surprised Sharni, with his mother looking younger than the forty she must have been at the time, with short dark hair and dancing dark eyes that sparkled with happiness. She was standing in a park somewhere, leaning against a tree, her hands curled lovingly over her rounded stomach.

'And this is me having my first bath,' Adrian pointed out. 'And, yes, you don't have to say it. I was a bit scrawny back then. But I was born a month early. See? This is me at three months, all filled out.'

Sharni didn't look at the photo of Adrian at three months. She was still frowning down at the photo of him having his first bath, and at the woman holding him in that bath. His mother. May.

A man might not have noticed her hair. But Sharni did. Straight away.

It wasn't short as it had been in the photo of her when she was six months pregnant. It was long, longer than shoulder-length.

Hair didn't grow that long in a couple of months. It wasn't a wig, either. You didn't buy a wig with strands of grey in it.

My God, she thought with a quiver of true shock. He *was* adopted. All her suspicions hadn't been unfounded. Adrian was Ray's twin brother. He had to be!

'Would you believe Sharni thought I was adopted?' Adrian said laughingly, and glanced up at his mother.

Sharni looked up too, her stomach contracting when she glimpsed the flash of fear in the woman's eyes.

'Why on earth would she think that?' May replied.

'Sharni was married once before,' Adrian rattled on, apparently oblivious of his mother's alarm. 'Her husband was tragically killed in a train derailment a few years ago.'

'How awful. I'm so sorry, Sharni. But I still don't understand why you would think my son was adopted.'

'It's because I'm her husband's physical double,' Adrian explained. 'He was adopted, you see. I'm so much like him that Sharni thought we might have been twins, separated at birth and adopted out to two different families.'

Maybe if his mother hadn't spilled her sherry into her lap, Adrian might have remained unaware of the truth. Sharni certainly hadn't been about to tell him the truth.

His freezing next to her, rather than going to his mother's aid, told the story. It was left to Sharni to jump up and help the flustered woman, taking the half-empty glass from her shaking hands and putting it to one side.

'I'm such a clumsy fool these days,' May said in one last desperate attempt to cover things up.

But it was futile.

'I *am* adopted, aren't I?'

Adrian's sharp words sliced through the air from where he'd remained sitting on the lounge, with that damning photo album still open on his lap.

Sharni saw the despair in his mother's eyes as they lifted to look at her son. 'No, Adrian, you're not.'

'Don't lie to me!' he snapped.

'I'm not lying. Your father and I… We didn't adopt you,' she said, her shoulders sagging in defeat. 'We stole you.'

CHAPTER TWENTY

ADRIAN STARED at his mother, then at Sharni, who was looking as shell-shocked as he was feeling.

'Stole me,' he repeated in a somewhat dazed tone. 'What do you mean you *stole* me?'

His mother slumped back down into her armchair, her head sinking down into her hands. 'I never thought you'd find out,' she cried. 'I can't believe this is happening.'

'Mum, for pity's sake, pull yourself together and tell me what you and Dad did.'

'Adrian, don't,' Sharni warned, and began stroking his mother gently around her shoulders. 'Can't you see she's upset?'

'*She's* upset!' he snapped, fury and confusion raging within him. 'What about me?'

Sharni's eyes were soft upon him. 'You're upset, too. But you're stronger than she is.'

'Am I?' He didn't feel strong at this moment. He felt shattered, the foundations of his life crumbling with his mother's stunning revelation.

'Yes,' Sharni said. 'You are.'

The conviction in her voice calmed him, as did the sympathy in her eyes.

'Mrs Palmer,' Sharni said gently, and knelt down beside his mother. 'You have to tell Adrian what happened. He needs to know the whole story.'

'He…he won't understand,' the woman sobbed.

'He will.'

Adrian wasn't sure that he would. But Sharni's belief in him was touching.

His eyes dropped back to the album still open on his lap, his anger quickly on the rise again.

'This photo of you pregnant,' he said, jabbing at it with his finger. 'Was that just a sham? Is that a pillow stuffed under there?'

His mother lifted her tear-stained face. 'No. That's me, really pregnant. I'd already suffered three miscarriages, but, this time, everything seemed to be going well. I…I went into labour shortly after that photo was taken. The baby died a few hours after he was born,' she finished in a bereft voice. 'A boy.'

'Go on.'

'There were complications, and I…I couldn't have another baby after that. I became seriously depressed. Your father…he…he was very worried about me.'

'So he went out and stole a baby for you? I can't believe he'd do that. Not Dad. He was such a stickler for doing the right thing. Hell, he brought me up on honesty is the best policy!'

'I knew you wouldn't understand,' his mother wailed.

'Adrian, don't,' Sharni said with a reproving glance.

'Don't what?' He threw the album to one side and stood up, unable to sit still any longer.

'Don't be cruel,' Sharni chided, but gently.

'It's all right, dear,' May said. 'He has a right to be angry.'

Angry? He was more than bloody angry. Adrian stalked around behind the sofa where he ground to a halt, his hands gripping the back with white-knuckled intensity.

'So how did it happen?' he demanded to know. 'Where did you steal me from? A hospital?'

'No! It wasn't like that at all,' his mother choked out. 'It wasn't intentional!'

'I just landed in your lap one day, is that it?'

His mother's sigh was ragged. 'No, of course not.'

Sharni shot him an exasperated look. 'Adrian, why don't you shut up and let your mother explain?'

Adrian threw up his hands in disgust. 'Fine. Explain away. If you can.'

'Oh, God,' his mother cried.

Sharni patted her hand. 'Just tell the truth, May.'

Adrian had to admire Sharni's gentle touch with his mother. Not that she was his *real* mother, he thought bitterly!

'I'll try, dear,' she said, and glanced nervously over at Adrian. 'At the time, your father had a medical practice in Sydney. In Surrey Hills. Not the most salubrious of areas, but you know how your father liked helping those less fortunate than himself. I hadn't worked since my baby died three years earlier. I couldn't. I…I came in to the city to meet your father for dinner one Friday evening. His receptionist had just left and he was closing the surgery when this young woman burst in, obviously in labour. It was too late to ring an ambulance, the baby already coming. I helped your father deliver you, not knowing at the time that there was a second baby as well. It all happened so quickly. We were shocked when a second baby arrived on the scene. The girl admitted she hadn't been to a doctor during her whole pregnancy, and had no idea she was having twins. Had no idea who the father of her babies were, either. She was a runaway and had been squatting in some derelict building up at the Cross. Arthur was attending to her afterbirth when she complained of a fierce headache. Within seconds she was dead. An aneurism had burst on her brain, we found out later. Suddenly, we had these two newborn babies in our arms.'

'And you decided to steal one,' Adrian said drily.

His mother winced, making Adrian feel momentarily guilty.

'Arthur was against the idea but he could see I was determined. I wanted to take both babies, but he said we would never get away with that. He said I had to choose.'

'Why me? Why not my brother?'

'You were a bit bigger. And stronger. And you didn't cry. Your brother. He never stopped. Arthur said a crying baby would bring unwanted attention. I took you home in a taxi whilst Arthur rang the police and ambulance, not telling them the girl had had twins. I still had everything I'd bought in preparation for our own baby boy. I couldn't bear to throw anything away. I packed everything that night and drove with you to Brisbane the following morning. I had an aunt there. Aunt Charlotte. My only living relative. You probably don't remember her. She died when you were only little. Anyway, I told her the truth and she kindly let me stay with her till Arthur settled things in Sydney. We knew we had to get away and start a new life where we could pretend you were our real baby. Luckily, Arthur didn't have any close relatives here in Australia who would ask awkward questions. As you know, he migrated from England when he was in his thirties. When his father died, his mother married a man he couldn't stand. He didn't write and they'd lost touch with each other.'

'What about friends?' Adrian asked. 'Didn't you have any friends who'd wonder where you'd gone? And why?'

'We hadn't socialised much since our baby died, due to my depression. So, no, we didn't have any close friends.'

Adrian found it difficult to take everything in. Suddenly, the need to get away by himself was acute. He had to think, had to try to come to terms with everything.

'If that's all, then I'm going to go for a walk,' he said abruptly.

'Adrian, no,' Sharni said. 'Don't do that.'

'It's all right,' his mother said. 'It's what he always does when he's upset.'

It irked him that she knew him this well, this woman who wasn't really his mother.

'One thing before I go,' he said sharply. 'Did you ever find out anything about my real mother?'

Again, that grimace of hurt. And again, more guilt.

'Arthur did make enquiries. She came from a wealthy Sydney family. But her parents didn't want anything to do with their illegitimate grandson. They quite happily signed the papers to allow for his adoption.'

Adrian could not believe he could be hurt by a rejection from people he didn't even know. But he was.

'I see,' he bit out. 'They wouldn't have wanted me either, then, would they?'

'*I* wanted you,' May said with a fierce love shining in her teary eyes. 'From the first moment I held you in my arms.'

Tears pricked at his own eyes, making him panic. He refused to cry in front of the woman he loved. Refused to let her see him as any less than the confident, self-assured man she'd fallen in love with.

But *had* she? came the sudden awful fear.

I am her husband's twin brother. Not just his double. I carry the same DNA. It fooled his dog. Has it fooled her, too? Is she mine for real, or have I just stepped into my brother's shoes?

The thought horrified him.

'If you'll excuse me, I need some time alone.'

CHAPTER TWENTY-ONE

'HE HATES me,' May said brokenly after Adrian left the house.

'No, he doesn't,' Sharni denied. 'He's in shock. But you were right about one thing. He doesn't understand what drove you to steal him. But I do, May. Honestly, I do. I know what it's like to lose a much-loved baby.'

'You do?'

'Yes. I was expecting when my husband was killed. The shock put me into premature labour and the baby died. A little boy.'

'Oh, Sharni. You poor love. At least I had Arthur to comfort me.'

'It was a very hard time for me,' Sharni admitted, surprised to find that she could talk about it now without dissolving into tears. She would never forget the pain of that time, but at last she was capable of moving on.

'What was he like?' May asked. 'Your husband, I mean. Adrian's brother.'

'He was a lovely man,' she said with fond memory.

'Very sweet, and gentle. But not all that confident in himself. Nothing like Adrian, except in looks. I think he might have been Adrian's mirror-image twin. You must know about that, being a nurse.'

'I've heard about it. Yes.'

'When I first saw Adrian I thought he was Ray's exact physical double. But after a while I could see little differences in his face. Then the other morning, I saw his reflection in the mirror and it was like Ray was looking straight at me.'

May shook her head. 'It's unbelievable that you should meet Adrian, don't you think? In a city with four million people, and you come across your husband's twin brother.'

'Maybe it was destiny. Or Ray up in heaven, directing me to the one man who could make me happy again.'

'And he has? Made you happy?'

'Very. Tell me, do you know where he might have gone?'

'He's sure to be down on the beach somewhere.'

'I'll go find him.'

May glanced down at her sherry-stained top. 'And I'll change, then see what I can do about keeping that dinner from spoiling.'

'Everything is going to be all right, May,' Sharni said with a reassuring smile. 'Adrian loves you very much. Nothing is ever going to change that.'

'I hope you're right, dear. It can't be easy, finding out something like this at his age. I could see it rocked him.'

'I know that, May. My husband, Ray…he never really came to terms with being adopted. He always suffered from a sense of abandonment.'

'But he wasn't abandoned!' she protested. 'His mother died. Wasn't he ever told that?'

'No. His adopted mother always told him he'd been given up because he wasn't wanted.'

'Oh, how dreadful!'

'She was a stupid, selfish woman. I never could take to her. After she died I encouraged Ray to find out the details of his adoption but he wouldn't. At least Adrian knows what really happened.'

'Yes, that's true.'

'I haven't told Adrian yet about the baby I lost. I think now is the right time. It might help him to understand why you did what you did.'

Tears glistened in May's eyes. 'And there I was, thinking how unlucky he was to meet you, of all people. But that's not true. My boy is very lucky to have you. You are just what he needs.'

Just what he needs.

May's words reverberated in Sharni's head as she walked down the road towards the beach.

Janice had been so right. That was what had been missing from her relationship with Adrian. The feeling of being needed.

She could not wait to go to him, to make him see that

he would survive this, that nothing of value in his life had changed. His mother still loved him, and so did she. More than ever.

Adrian felt her presence before she sat down beside him on the sand. He didn't turn to look at her, just continued to stare out at the sea.

'Okay, so you were right and I was wrong,' he bit out. 'I am your dead husband's twin brother.'

'Yes,' she said quite calmly. 'You are.'

Now his head did whip round, his eyes stabbing resentment at her. 'Doesn't that bother you at all?'

She blinked genuine surprise at him. 'No.'

'Well, it bothers me.'

'Why?'

'If you have to ask then you don't understand men at all.'

'Ray wouldn't mind, Adrian.'

'*I* mind. You're his wife. You loved *him* first. I come a poor second.'

'That's not true,' she said firmly. 'Yes. I did love Ray. But I love you just as much.'

He shook his head at her, still unconvinced. 'I don't want to live my life in another's man's shoes.'

'It's impossible for you to do that, Adrian. If you'd known Ray, you would see how different you are from him.'

'Well, I didn't know my brother, did I? I was denied

that chance when my darling mother stole me. Not that she's my real mother.'

Adrian was startled by the outrage that zoomed into Sharni's eyes. 'Don't you dare say that! May is your real mother, just as your father was your real father. They gave you everything a child could hope for. Love, security, a good education and lots of self-esteem. Ray didn't have much of that, I can assure you.'

'He might have, if we'd been kept together,' he said stubbornly.

'Maybe. Maybe not. I suspect he might have always been in your shadow. You were the stronger twin, Adrian. But what's done is done and it can't be changed. We're all victims of circumstance, especially when we're children. But once we become adults, we have choices. You can choose to be bitter and resentful over a decision you had no part in thirty-six years ago. Or you can choose to be understanding and forgiving.'

'That's all very well for you to say, Sharni. But how can I be understanding when I simply *don't* understand? Not every woman who loses a child goes around and steals someone else's.'

'No,' she said. 'But your mother hadn't just lost one child, Adrian. She'd already lost three. On top of that, she'd been given the news that she could never have another.'

'They could have adopted. Through the right channels,' he added caustically.

'They were too old to be considered.'

'Not if they'd gone overseas.'

'Thirty-six years ago? Come on, Adrian, no one did that back then.'

'You still don't steal a child.'

'She didn't plan to, Adrian. Fate stepped in and put a terrible temptation in your mother's path. She simply couldn't say no.'

'Dad should have said no.'

'He couldn't. Not if he loved her as much as he obviously did.'

Adrian nodded reluctantly. 'He adored her.'

'And they both adored you. That can't be a bad thing, can it?'

A rush of air escaped Adrian's lungs as he let go of some of the tension gripping his insides. 'No. They were wonderful parents,' he admitted. 'But it's just all so unbelievable.'

'You've had a big shock,' she said.

His smile was wan. 'That's putting it mildly.'

But she was right, Adrian conceded. About everything. He was being irrational and emotional. Still, it was hard not to be.

'You know that room in my house which I wouldn't let you go into? The one next to the bathroom.'

Adrian frowned at Sharni's abrupt change of subject. When he turned his head to look at her, she wasn't looking at him, her eyes straight ahead.

'Yes,' he replied somewhat hesitantly, because there

was something in her body language that worried him. 'What about it?'

'It's a nursery,' she told him.

'A nursery,' he repeated.

'Yes. A blue one.'

'A blue one.'

'It was never used,' she said. 'But it had everything. A cradle and a cot, with a mobile hanging over it, plus a change table and more clothes than any baby could ever wear.'

Only then did she turn to look at him, her chin quivering slightly. 'I was five and a half months pregnant when Ray died. The shock sent me into labour and my son wasn't old enough to live.'

Oh, God. The poor darling.

'I *know* the pain your mother felt, Adrian. It tears you apart then leaves you feeling dead inside. You brought her to life again. That was why she couldn't let you go. That was why she had to keep you. *I* was dead inside for five long years. But then you came along and brought me to life again in a way I never thought possible.'

She reached out and lay a soft hand against his cheek.

'You are not a substitute for Ray. You are you, Adrian Palmer, and I love you more than words can describe. You asked me to marry you on the way up here. If that offer is still open, then my answer is yes.'

As Adrian looked deep into her eyes all his emotional confusion fell away, replaced by the absolute certainty that she was telling him the truth. She loved him. Truly loved *him*.

What an incredible woman she was. After all she'd been through, she was still capable of facing life with courage and optimism. Still capable of loving.

He pulled her into his arms and held her tightly against him.

'You make me feel humble,' he said. 'I don't deserve you.'

A wonderful peace filled Sharni's soul as Adrian held her. It had been so good to finally tell him about the baby. Now, there were no secrets between them. Only love.

'I'll make you happy,' he promised her as he pressed his lips into her hair.

'You already have. Come on, let's go back and have that dinner your mother very kindly cooked us.'

'I hurt her, didn't I?' Adrian said as they walked, hand in hand, up the hill.

'Nothing that a big hug won't fix,' Sharni replied. 'Mothers are very forgiving people.'

'She's been a brilliant mother, really,' he admitted.

Talking of mothers brought his mind back to the child Sharni had lost. Clearly, having a baby would mean a lot to her.

I'll give you another baby, my darling, he vowed privately, his fingers squeezing hers. Or I'll die trying.

CHAPTER TWENTY-TWO

ADRIAN could not sit at his desk any longer. His mind was not on his work, his ability to concentrate totally shot.

Pushing back his chair, he stood up and made his way from his study to the kitchen where he poured himself some coffee. A glance at his watch showed it had just gone noon. Sharni's appointment with the specialist had been for ten-thirty. Surely she would be finished by now. He'd asked her to call him as soon as she could, but his phone remained silent.

Five weeks had gone by since their memorable trip to Kingscliff, more than enough time for Adrian to buy Sharni an extremely expensive engagement ring, then start making plans for a wedding before the end of the year.

He hadn't convinced her to move in with him as yet, Sharni insisting that she stay in Katoomba till her place was sold. She did, however, come down every weekend, which she said was easier than his coming up to her.

Mozart had found a new home at her sister's place—

he'd become very attached to Janice's two boys—so leaving him behind wasn't a problem any more.

Meanwhile, Adrian had set about getting his fiancée an appointment with the best fertility expert in Sydney, a task that had taken longer than he'd hoped. The infernal man had been overseas till recently.

The sound of the front door opening sent his heart racing and him hurrying towards the foyer.

It was Sharni, of course, looking her usual lovely self in his favourite black trousers and pink jumper. Her cheeks were pink as well, her dark eyes sparkling with what he hoped was good news.

'You naughty girl,' he said, bending to give her a peck on the cheek. 'Why didn't you ring? I've been like a cat on a hot tin roof this last half-hour.'

'Sorry. I didn't want to ring. I wanted to tell you what the doctor said personally.'

'You look happy, so I take it it isn't bad news.'

'It's wonderful news.'

'Your ovaries are working again?'

She smiled. 'It seems so.'

He frowned. 'But you still haven't had a period.'

'Funny that, isn't it?' she said, looking impossibly smug.

The penny dropped and his pulse rate took off.

'You're already pregnant,' he said breathlessly.

She squealed an excited, 'Yes,' then threw herself into his arms.

Adrian could hardly believe their luck.

'How far gone are you?' he asked.

'He said about six weeks.'

'That means…'

'Yes. I must have conceived the very first weekend we were together.'

'That's incredible.'

'No, I think it's perfectly credible. I told you you made me come alive again. You did, in the most marvellous way. Oh, but I love you, Adrian Palmer,' she said, and hugged him tightly once more, her head resting over his heart.

Adrian sighed with happiness. This was what he'd vowed to do, what he wanted most in the world. Because this was what *she* wanted, this beautiful, brave woman he loved.

Every time he started feeling down or upset about the circumstances of his birth—which happened more often than he'd anticipated—he would think of Sharni, and all she'd had to endure.

Her wise advice would come back to him about making adult choices instead of indulging in negative emotions.

I choose not to be angry, he would tell himself. Or judgemental. I choose to go forward and make the best of my life.

Which was what he was doing.

And now he was going to be a father.

How lucky could he get!

'Maybe we should ring Janice,' Sharni said, her head lifting. 'And your mum. Tell them the good news.'

'I think they can wait a few minutes, don't you?' he said. 'I want to savour this moment with just you. Come on, let's go open a bottle of champagne.'

'Uh-uh,' she said, shaking her head. 'No alcohol for mums-to-be.'

He smiled. 'Coffee, then? I have some perking in the kitchen.'

'Sounds good.'

'You simply have to move in with me now,' he said once they retreated to the terrace, mugs in hand. 'I want to look after you. I'm also going to have to design and build us a house. Can't raise a family in this place. Tell you what, there's no need to sell your place at all. Let's just rent it out. That way you can move in with me this week.'

'Okay,' she said, seeming happy with that idea.

'But you're not to pack. I'll hire a company to do all that.'

'If you insist.'

'I insist.'

She glanced at him over the rim of her mug. 'I can see that your son is going to be a real bossy-boots.'

'What makes you think it'll be a boy?' he said.

Sharni looked at the man she loved, and smiled. 'Intuition.'

She was right. Their first-born was a boy. But he wasn't a bossy-boots at all. He was an easygoing child who loved animals and music.

He was named Raymond Arthur, but everyone called him Ray.

Undressed
BY THE BOSS

From sensible suits…into satin sheets!

Stranded in a Nevada hotel, Kate throws herself
on the mercy of hotelier Zack Boudreaux.
In exchange for a job and a way home, he'll
make her his very personal assistant….

THE TYCOON'S VERY
PERSONAL ASSISTANT
by Heidi Rice
Book # 2761

Available in September:

If you love stories about a gorgeous boss, look out for:

BUSINESS IN THE
BEDROOM
by Anne Oliver
Book # 2770

Available next month in Harlequin Presents.

I ♥ HARLEQUIN *Presents*

BROUGHT TO YOU BY FANS OF
HARLEQUIN PRESENTS.

We are its editors and authors
and biggest fans—and we'd
love to hear from YOU!

Subscribe today to our online blog at
www.iheartpresents.com

SPECIAL EDITION™

NEW YORK TIMES BESTSELLING AUTHOR

DIANA PALMER

A brand-new Long, Tall Texans novel

HEART OF STONE

Feeling unwanted and unloved, Keely returns to Jacobsville and to Boone Sinclair, a rancher troubled by his own past. Boone has always seemed reserved, but now Keely discovers a sensuality with him that quickly turns to love. Can they each see past their own scars to let love in?

*Available September 2008
wherever you buy books.*

REQUEST YOUR FREE BOOKS!

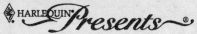 HARLEQUIN *Presents* ®

2 FREE NOVELS
PLUS 2
FREE GIFTS!

YES! Please send me 2 FREE Harlequin Presents® novels and my 2 FREE gifts (gifts are worth about $10). After receiving them, if I don't wish to receive any more books, I can return the shipping statement marked "cancel". If I don't cancel, I will receive 6 brand-new novels every month and be billed just $4.05 per book in the U.S. or $4.74 per book in Canada, plus 25¢ shipping and handling per book and applicable taxes, if any*. That's a savings of close to 15% off the cover price! I understand that accepting the 2 free books and gifts places me under no obligation to buy anything. I can always return a shipment and cancel at any time. Even if I never buy another book, the two free books and gifts are mine to keep forever.

106 HDN ERRW   306 HDN ERRL

Name	(PLEASE PRINT)
Address	Apt. #
City	State/Prov.	Zip/Postal Code

Signature (if under 18, a parent or guardian must sign)

Mail to the **Harlequin Reader Service:**
IN U.S.A.: P.O. Box 1867, Buffalo, NY 14240-1867
IN CANADA: P.O. Box 609, Fort Erie, Ontario L2A 5X3

Not valid to current subscribers of Harlequin Presents books.

Want to try two free books from another line?
Call 1-800-873-8635 or visit www.morefreebooks.com.

* Terms and prices subject to change without notice. N.Y. residents add applicable sales tax. Canadian residents will be charged applicable provincial taxes and GST. Offer not valid in Quebec. This offer is limited to one order per household. All orders subject to approval. Credit or debit balances in a customer's account(s) may be offset by any other outstanding balance owed by or to the customer. Please allow 4 to 6 weeks for delivery. Offer available while quantities last.

Your Privacy: Harlequin Books is committed to protecting your privacy. Our Privacy Policy is available online at www.eHarlequin.com or upon request from the Reader Service. From time to time we make our lists of customers available to reputable third parties who may have a product or service of interest to you. If you would prefer we not share your name and address, please check here. ☐

HP08R

Inside ROMANCE

Stay up-to-date on all your romance reading news!

The Inside Romance newsletter is a FREE quarterly newsletter highlighting our upcoming series releases and promotions!

Click on the <u>Inside Romance</u> link on the front page of **www.eHarlequin.com** or e-mail us at insideromance@harlequin.ca to sign up to receive your FREE newsletter today!

You can also subscribe by writing us at: HARLEQUIN BOOKS Attention: Customer Service Department P.O. Box 9057, Buffalo, NY 14269-9057

Please allow 4-6 weeks for delivery of the first issue by mail.

IRNBPA108